"You Know ⟨...⟩ Here, Don't You?"

Shep asked.

"Yes," Andrea whispered. He was going to kiss her, and she rose on tiptoes to bring their lips closer together.

That was all Shep could take. His mouth covered hers in a kiss of utter possession. His hands roamed her back and hips.

"Shep...oh, Shep," she managed to whisper raggedly between the second and third kiss.

Then she lost count. She was barely aware of being backed up against a wall, and only dimly cognizant of him sliding her skirt up and then lifting one of her legs to wind it around his hips.

"Tell me you want this," he demanded gruffly, hoarsely.

Her lips were parted to take in gasping breaths. "How can you doubt it?"

"Tell me. Say it."

"I want it. I want *you*."

Dear Reader,

Happy holidays from the staff at Silhouette Desire! As you can see by the special cover treatment this month, these books are our holiday gifts to you. And each and every story is so wonderful that I know you'll want to buy extras to give to your friends!

We begin with Jackie Merritt's MAN OF THE MONTH, *Montana Christmas*, which is the conclusion of her spectacular MADE IN MONTANA series. The fun continues with *Instant Dad*, the final installment in Raye Morgan's popular series THE BABY SHOWER.

Suzannah Davis's *Gabriel's Bride* is a classic— and sensuous—love story you're sure to love. And Anne Eames's delightful writing style is highlighted to perfection in *Christmas Elopement*. For a story that will make you feel all the warmth and goodwill of the holiday season, don't miss Kate Little's *Jingle Bell Baby*.

And Susan Connell begins a new miniseries— THE GIRLS MOST LIKELY TO... —about three former high school friends who are now all grown up in *Rebel's Spirit*. Look for upcoming books in the series in 1997.

Happy holidays and happy reading from

Lucia Macro

AND THE STAFF OF SILHOUETTE DESIRE

Please address questions and book requests to:
Silhouette Reader Service
U.S.: 3010 Walden Ave., P.O. Box 1325, Buffalo, NY 14269
Canadian: P.O. Box 609, Fort Erie, Ont. L2A 5X3

JACKIE
MERRITT
MONTANA CHRISTMAS

SILHOUETTE *Desire*®
Published by Silhouette Books
America's Publisher of Contemporary Romance

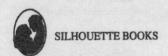

SILHOUETTE BOOKS

ISBN 0-373-76039-6

MONTANA CHRISTMAS

Books by Jackie Merritt

JACKIE MERRITT

and her husband live just outside Las Vegas, Nevada. An accountant for many years, Jackie has happily traded numbers for words. Next to family, books are her greatest joy. She started writing in 1987 and her efforts paid off in 1988 with the publication of her first novel. When she's not writing or enjoying a good book, Jackie dabbles in watercolor painting and likes playing the piano in her spare time.

FANON FAMILY TREE

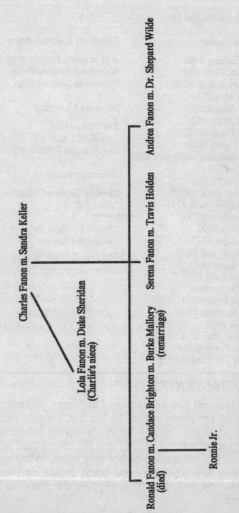

Charles Fanon m. Sandra Keller

Lola Fanon m. Duke Sheridan
(Charlie's niece)

Ronald Fanon m. Candace Brighton m. Burke Mallory
(died)   (remarriage)

Serena Fanon m. Travis Holden

Andrea Fanon m. Dr. Shepard Wilde

Ronnie Jr.

MONTANA FEVER (Desire #1014) = Lola and Duke's story
MONTANA PASSION (Special Edition #1051) = Serena and Travis's story
MONTANA LOVERS (Special Edition #1065) = Candace and Burke's story
MONTANA CHRISTMAS (Desire #1039) = Andrea and Shep's story

One

The town of Rocky Ford, Montana, was picture-postcard pretty on this wintry December morning. An eight-inch blanket of snow sparkled in the bright morning sun, shining from a sky so blue it made Andrea Dillon's eyes water to look at it. Wearing dark glasses against the glare, and dressed in warm clothing, she began shoveling out her driveway.

The air was cold and invigorating, bringing color to her cheeks. Her exhaled breath came out of her mouth in puffy little clouds. She had to smile, if a bit wryly; the long driveway had been one of the features of her rental house that had pleased her so much. This was the first major snowfall since she had moved in last summer, and she was certainly going to rack up her quota, and more, of exercise today by clearing the driveway enough to get her car to the street.

But being outside on such an incredible day felt wonderful. Other than at ski resorts in California, she had never seen snow like this. Her front lawn looked as smooth as a sheet of paper. The top of each bush and shrub was shaped into a rounded snow-bump. Every branch and twig on the leafless trees seemed artistically layered with a coat of glistening snow. The roof of her house looked as though someone had iced it with white frosting.

Lucas Wilde's roof, too, looked decorated with icing, Andrea thought with a fond glance at the one home she could see from her driveway in the sparsely populated neighborhood. Lucas was several years past sixty, Andrea estimated, and her best friend in this small town. Her *only* friend, she amended quickly.

Sighing softly, she began shoveling again.

"Andrea! Good morning!"

Recognizing Lucas's voice, she turned to smile at him as he walked toward her from the street. He was carrying a shovel. "Hi, Lucas. Isn't this a glorious morning?"

Lucas's rolling laugh rang out. "It is if you enjoy shoveling snow. I've already done my driveway and sidewalks, and now I'm going to help with yours."

"Lucas, that's not at all necessary."

"Course it's not." Lucas grinned. "Big, strapping girl like you could shovel for three days and not get winded."

Andrea had to laugh. She was definitely not "big and strapping." In fact, she was on the small side, barely five foot four inches tall and weighing in around one-ten.

"I might not be big," she retorted pertly, teasing him as he was teasing her, "but I'm strong."

Lucas laughed again. Compared to his six-foot-two height and two-hundred-forty-pound weight, she was a little bit of a person, and her proclamation of physical strength was obviously funny to him.

"But how much snow have you shoveled before?" he asked. "I'll bet this is your first time."

"Okay, so I've never shoveled snow before today. But I'm truly enjoying the job. Lucas, since you've already cleared your own driveway and sidewalks, you're probably tired. Please don't overdo it by helping me." She worried about Lucas at times. He was at least forty pounds overweight, carrying most of the excess poundage in his chest and belly. If he had a heart attack shoveling her driveway, she would never forgive herself.

"For your information, young woman, I'm not tired and I'm not ready to go back inside. I'll shovel a bit more, if you don't mind." Lucas set to work.

He sure could be stubborn when he wanted to be, Andrea thought. Stubborn in a nice way, though. Giving up on the friendly debate, she dug her own shovel into the snow. "Did you hear the storm in the night?"

"Sure did. Thought the wind was going to blow the roof off for a while there."

"I loved hearing it. There's something about a storm at night that makes me feel cozy and safe."

"It does that, all right. Makes one think of his own good fortune—having a warm bed, comfortable home, enough financial security to get by without worrying all the time. Not everyone's so lucky."

"True," Andrea agreed, frowning a little. Her financial security was not of her making. As she bent and scooped at a brisk tempo, her thoughts went to her mother. Sandra had died last February, and Andrea had been the only recipient of her estate. It was shortly after the funeral, when she'd been given access to her mother's private papers, that the series of events began that had changed the course of her life. She'd been working for the *Los Angeles Times,* still an unimportant cog in the production of the huge newspaper but harboring a longtime dream of journalistic success. Going through Sandra's papers, tying them together and finally grasping their import had been a shock. More of a shock, in fact, than her mother's sudden demise had been.

All of her life, she had believed her father to be the man named on her birth certificate: Harry Dillon. Harry was a total mystery to her. Sandra had waved the subject aside as trivial every time Andrea had tried to talk about him, as though it didn't matter that her daughter's father never visited, never called, never even sent birthday cards. Because of several documents in her mother's files, Andrea had deemed it essential to finally meet Harry Dillon. She'd hired a detective agency to locate him, which proved surprisingly easy to do. Then, armed with those documents, she'd paid Harry a visit.

He was a cordial man, married many years with grown children. After a little prodding and an explanation of her curiosity, Andrea had finally learned the facts of her own life.

"Your mother was pregnant with you when we got married, Andrea. She was pregnant when she went to Nevada to obtain a quickie divorce from your real father, a man called Charles Fanon. No, I have no idea where you might find Mr. Fanon. I agreed to my name being used on your birth certificate, as I was very smitten by Sandra and would have agreed to anything she asked."

Harry had smiled ruefully. "But she never loved me, and proved it by leaving me before you were a year old. I'm sorry you had to grow up thinking your father didn't want you, but the truth was that Sandra wouldn't permit even the slightest contact. Apparently, when she was done with a man, that was it."

Andrea's own memory had reinforced Harry's comment. Counting Charles A. Fanon—she had the divorce papers between Sandra and Charles as proof of Harry's story—Sandra had been married five times. And yes, when she was through with a man, she wouldn't even speak to him on the phone. As Sandra's last three husbands had all been wealthy men, Andrea could only surmise that her mother had married Harry, a common laborer, to legitimize her unborn child. In spite of Sandra's many missteps and indiscretions with men, she had possessed an innate sense of propriety. In fact, even while she was flitting from man to man—she hadn't married them all—one would have been hard-pressed to label her anything but a lady.

Anyhow, the same detective agency that had located Harry had tracked Charles Fanon to Rocky Ford, Montana. Andrea had quit her job, left her mother's very nice house—which now belonged to Andrea—in the hands of a trustworthy couple who had been in Sandra's employ for many years, and traveled to Rocky Ford with every intention of immediately confronting Mr. Fanon. Once there, however, her courage had deserted her, and after seven months, she was still procrastinating.

At times, she was furious with herself for delaying something she knew had to be done. At others, she rationalized her cowardice by concentrating on the things she had learned about Charles—or Charlie, as he was called in Rocky Ford. For one, she wasn't his only family. He had a daughter, Serena Holden, and a niece, Lola Sheridan. Also, there had been a son, Ronald, who had died in the military. Ronald's widow, Candace, and their young son, Ronnie, had lived with Charlie until Candace remarried. Candace's new husband, Burke Mallory, was the only person in Montana who knew Andrea's background. Burke was now a cattle rancher, but he'd been a cop on an undercover investigation in Rocky Ford when he'd run into Andrea under suspicious circumstances. It had taken him only a few days to unearth her true identity, which had greatly upset Andrea until Burke promised her that he would not reveal her secret to anyone. She had enormous respect for Burke Mallory, but was glad his and Candace's ranch was eighty miles from town, which pretty much eliminated chance meetings.

As for Charlie, he'd been living alone in his big old house on Foxworth Street since Candace and Burke's wedding. Andrea often wondered if he was lonely now, although he did have a coffee shop in the front portion of his house to keep him busy. Every night while lying in her bed before falling asleep, she pictured herself walking into that coffee shop and introducing herself. *Hello, Charlie. I'm Andrea Dillon, your third child, your second daughter.* She usually went to sleep with a sickish feeling in her stomach because of that fantasy.

And maybe that's all the whole thing was, she was beginning to think—a fantasy. If Charlie hadn't wanted a third child at the time of his and her mother's divorce, why on earth would he want one now? Why was she so driven to see this through and, at the same time, too cowardly to do it? *Why* was she afraid? She hadn't been afraid to call

on Harry, after all. Maybe *leery* was a better word for
whatever it was inside of her that kept her from accom-
plishing her goal with Charlie. But if she was never going
to confront him, why stay in this small Montana town?

These were not new questions. Andrea had been asking
them of herself for months, without being able to supply
the answers. Surprising her, however, was an answer about
why she stayed in Rocky Ford: she liked it there. For the
first time in her life, she was putting down roots. Sandra
had moved them around California so much, Andrea had
never felt connected to any one place. Here, in this unpre-
tentious little country town, she was at long last discover-
ing the tranquillity of belonging.

Even so, she wasn't entirely content. There was Charlie,
of course, almost constantly on her mind, and she knew
liking a town was no excuse for living a purposeless existence. A job might do wonders for the doldrums she often
suffered, and hopefully tire her enough to make her sleep
better. At the very least, she would have something to think
about besides the Fanon family.

Lucas broke into her somber thoughts. "Ready for
Christmas, Andrea? It's not far off now, you know."

Andrea stuck her shovel into the snow and then leaned
on it. She was neither ready for Christmas nor thrilled that
the holiday season was upon her. Looking at Lucas's
pleasant face, ruddy from the cold, she wondered how to
answer his question. He knew very little of her background, mere bits and pieces that she had thought were safe
enough to pass on. One brief conversation had been about
the death of her mother.

She fell back on that. "With Mother gone, I'm afraid
I'm not feeling very much holiday cheer, Lucas."

He stopped shoveling and conveyed embarrassment by
clearing his throat. "Course you're not. I shouldn't have
mentioned it."

Guilt struck Andrea. Sandra had rarely spent Christmas
with her. Instead, she was off to the Bahamas, or Ber-
muda, or somewhere else elegant and sunny, with one man
or another. Andrea's Christmases had usually been spent

with some of Sandra's friends or with servants. That was during her childhood, of course. Once she was old enough to make her own decisions, she chose which of her own friends with whom she wanted to celebrate the holiday.

The truth was that Christmas simply didn't excite her. It never had.

But it seemed important to Lucas, and he, too, was alone. His only offspring was a son living in Los Angeles, an extremely successful plastic surgeon, happily married, according to Lucas, and too busy to come home for the holidays.

"Lucas, do you have any plans for Christmas Day?" she asked.

He looked off into the distance, appearing wistful to Andrea. "I'll probably do what I usually do, drop in on a few friends."

"Would you like to have dinner with me?"

His head came around. "I don't want to impose, Andrea."

"You wouldn't be imposing. You'd be doing me a favor. I've been planning to cook a turkey with all the trimmings, and eating it alone wouldn't be any fun." She'd been planning no such thing, but once out of her mouth, it seemed like the best idea she'd had in a long time.

A smile broke out on Lucas's face. "Since you put it that way, yes, I'd love having Christmas dinner with you. Thanks for the invite."

Andrea smiled, too. "You're very welcome. Hey, guess what? I'm suddenly looking forward to Christmas." She realized it was true and smiled again as she started shoveling. She would even buy Lucas a present, nothing that would embarrass him because he didn't have one for her. Just some little thing she could put under the tree.

A tree? she thought with some amazement. My goodness, she really was getting into the holiday spirit, wasn't she? Well, why not? She and Lucas could have a very nice day together, and neither of them would be alone and despondent.

She thought of Lucas's son, Dr. Shepler Wilde, who was too busy to visit his aging father on Christmas, and snorted derisively. He was probably a self-centered, inconsiderate, better-than-thou jerk.

Maybe she could give Lucas a merry Christmas. It wouldn't completely make up for his son's negligence, but it would help.

By that evening, Andrea had to admit she was really looking forward to Christmas Day. If nothing else, planning a holiday dinner took her mind off the Fanons. Ready for bed, with her dark auburn hair damp from a shower and wearing her nightgown and robe, she curled up in her favorite chair with a pad and pen to prepare a grocery list. Even though she wouldn't be shopping for the ingredients for another week or so, she liked the idea of early organization.

The list grew quickly, but after a while she had to stop to think about it. As she did, her gaze drifted around her cozy living room and ultimately fell on a black-bound notebook tucked into a small bookcase along with several dozen books, all of which she had purchased and read since coming to Rocky Ford. Her thoughts immediately turned from her grocery list to the contents of that notebook. Everything she knew about the Fanon family was in it, including handwritten notes describing her own observations and every newspaper article mentioning the Fanons she had run across in the *Rocky Ford News*, which she had neatly clipped and pasted on various pages. Her last entry was a newspaper accounting of Candace Fanon and Burke Mallory's wedding. Burke had invited her to attend the affair, and she had wanted to go very badly. But she'd stayed away, knowing how uncomfortable she would be with Burke aware of her lurking in corners and spying on the Fanons, as she had done on several previous occasions when she'd been able to hide in a crowd. Then, however, no one had known who she was.

That notebook disturbed her, blatantly reminding her that she was on the outside looking in, yet she couldn't get rid of it. It was the most detailed documentation of any portion of her life, and destroying it would be like destroying a piece of herself.

Sighing with a profound sense of unrest, she forced herself to concentrate on Christmas dinner again.

For someone who had initially tried to ignore the holiday season, Andrea became very involved in it. Happy about it, too. She shopped for Lucas's present in Rocky Ford's stores, and enjoyed seeing the decorations the town had put up. Several businesses had outside speakers playing Christmas music, and every window in every shop was bright with holiday displays.

On impulse, she went into the drugstore and spent an hour picking out Christmas cards to send to the friends she had left behind in California. Leaving without a goodbye hadn't bothered her at the time; her mind had been overloaded with grief over her mother's death and the shocks that had come after. But, in retrospect, her hasty, unannounced departure seemed terribly rude, particularly so with the man she had been dating, Hale Jackson. Not that theirs had been a serious relationship. Hale was an aspiring actor, as vain as they came and too involved in his career to give any woman top billing. But he knew a lot of people and had been fun to go out with. She picked out an especially nice card for Hale. She also bought a load of decorations for the tree she planned to purchase when she was finished with her other shopping.

It surprised Andrea to walk past the Men's Western Wear store a few minutes later and see a sign in the window among a nativity scene and various Christmas decorations. It said, in bold print, Under New Management.

Lola Sheridan, Charlie's niece, must have sold her store, Andrea thought with a small frown. The Fanons managed to always stay one step ahead of her, forever altering or changing their status in some way. Those changes shouldn't disturb her peace of mind, but they did. The Fanons seemed to be a close-knit family, and maybe that was why she couldn't bring herself to barge in and boldly pronounce herself to be one of them.

Of course, she'd known nothing of Charlie's family when she first got to town, and she'd done no bold announcing then, either. The truth, bitter as it was to accept, was that she was a spineless wimp when it came to Charlie. And it hurt because she wanted to meet the father she'd never known so much she ached from it. She wanted him to open his heart to her, to welcome her into the family.

But would he?

Swallowing the sudden lump in her throat, she hurried on past the Men's Western Wear store, returned to her car parked down the street and got in.

But she wouldn't let herself rush home to lick her wounds, as she had done so many times in the past months. Rather, she bravely lifted her chin and drove to the vacant lot on which someone was selling Christmas trees.

The area had gone through several thaws and snowfalls since that first storm, and Andrea's yard was patchy with old snow and bare ground. It pleased her to see softly falling snow on Christmas Day.

By noon, she had everything well under control for a one-o'clock dinner. She had told Lucas they would eat early, watch old movies on TV, which she knew he liked, then have turkey sandwiches and leftovers for supper. Lucas had seemed thrilled with her plans, and she expected him to come knocking on her door at any minute.

She had dressed festively for the day, choosing a striking dress and high-heeled pumps in the same emerald green color and gold jewelry. Anytime she wore green, her eyes appeared more green than gray, and the color also brought out the red in her dark auburn hair. Feeling good because she looked good and was going to have company for dinner, she puttered in the kitchen with an ear cocked for Lucas's arrival.

When the phone rang at twelve-fifteen, she nearly jumped out of her skin. Rarely did her phone ring. Other than Lucas, no one in Rocky Ford had her unlisted number. But why would he be calling today? "Maybe it's one of those bothersome salespeople," she muttered under her breath as she walked over to the kitchen extension and picked it up with a cool, unapproachable "Hello?"

"Andrea, this is Lucas. Um...something's come up." Lucas uttered what sounded like a nervous laugh to Andrea, and her heart sank. Surely he wasn't going to tell her that he wasn't coming. The house was permeated with good smells from the turkey roasting in the oven and the other dishes she had prepared, the tree had turned out so pretty with its twinkling lights and tinsel, and she was so emotionally ready for a genuine Christmas celebration that disappointment was already digging its claws into her.

"Is something wrong, Lucas?" She tried to speak normally, but she was so afraid he was going to cancel coming to dinner that she sounded forlorn. Wincing at her childishness, she added in a stronger voice, "What came up, Lucas? Are you all right?"

"Heck, it's not me, honey. It's Shep."

Shep? Who or what was a Shep? "I don't understand, Lucas."

"Shep, Andrea, my son. He got here about thirty minutes ago. We've been unloading his car ever since. Mighty fine surprise it was to open my door and see him standing there. But...well, I'm a mite confused about the day now. I mean, you're expecting one guest and—"

Andrea broke in. An enormous sense of relief made her sound breathless. "Lucas, I have enough food prepared for ten people. By all means, bring your son with you."

"You're a sweet lady, Andrea. That's what I was hoping you'd say, and I was pretty sure you would, too. What I'm not sure of is if Shep will agree to go with me. I'm calling from my bedroom while he's doing some unpacking. Had his car loaded to the roof. Must have brought every stitch he owns. You see, he's here without his wife. Ex-wife, I should say." Lucas's voice had taken on a saddened note. "They're divorced, Andrea, and Shep's not very happy about it."

"Oh, dear," Andrea murmured sympathetically. "It happened awfully fast, didn't it?"

"Apparently not. Shep just never said anything to me about their troubles when we talked on the phone. I thought everything was great with them. I still don't know what really took place, but as I said, he's only been here about a half hour. Anyhow, you're sure it's okay to bring him along?"

"Of course I'm sure. I'll put another place setting on the table, Lucas. Do your best to convince Shep to come, and I'll do my best to make him feel welcome."

"Thanks, Andrea. You're a peach."

She put down the phone, realizing that Lucas had not said he would come even if Shep wouldn't. With a helpless sensation, she looked around her small but efficient kitchen. The house had come furnished, but she had added her own pretty touches to it, making it hers. Today the counter was loaded with food, and so was the refrigerator. Telling Lucas that she had enough to feed ten people had been only a slight exaggeration. Easily she could feed six or seven.

And if Lucas didn't come and help her eat some of it...?

Resentment for a man she'd never met suddenly assailed her. It was only natural for Lucas to be thrilled to see his son, but Dr. Shepler Wilde just showing up on his father's doorstep on Christmas Day with no warning whatsoever seemed darned inconsiderate to her. Would it have killed him to stop at some point in his journey north to call his father? For that matter, since his marital troubles weren't all that sudden, he could have informed Lucas weeks ago of his situation, and that he was coming home for Christmas.

He was probably exactly the kind of man she'd thought of before—an arrogant, self-centered jerk. And with a wonderful man like Lucas for a father, too. Andrea's lips thinned in potent disapproval. She had desperately yearned for her own father for as long as she could remember, and Shep Wilde treated his like dirt. Life certainly wasn't fair.

Well, she had no choice but to finish making dinner. There were potatoes to mash and gravy to make. If Lucas came, wonderful. If he didn't...?

"Merry Christmas," she mumbled as she set to work while battling a surge of self-pity. She wallowed in it for a few minutes, then cast it aside. She wouldn't die from eating alone, and she could watch her movies alone, as well. Maybe she'd take a walk in the snow after dinner. It was coming down in huge, fluffy flakes, once again turning her yard into a wintry fairyland.

Determinedly she marched into the living room and inserted a disk into her CD player, a gift she had bought for herself. Christmas music wafted from the speakers, and she adjusted the volume so she could hear it in the kitchen. Then she returned to her cooking.

Such was life, she thought with a sigh as she stirred the gravy. Rather, such was *her* life, she amended in the next breath. After all, if she wasn't such a flaming coward, she might be spending Christmas with Charlie and the rest of the Fanons.

Maybe she deserved to eat alone.

Intent on her own thoughts, she was startled to hear someone knocking on the back door. "Lucas," she said with instantaneous relief and excitement. He had come, after all. Whether his son was with him or not was immaterial. Lucas was here, and that was all that mattered.

Hurrying to the door, she pulled it open. It was Lucas, all right, and he wasn't alone. Standing just a little behind was the most handsome man Andrea had ever seen. As tall as his father, Dr. Shepler Wilde was lean where Lucas was heavy. His hair was thick and black and stunningly attractive with snowflakes in it. She assessed him quickly. Wide shoulders in a black leather jacket. Long legs in faded jeans. A white turtleneck sweater. Naturally dark-toned skin. A chiseled, sexy mouth. A strong chin and high cheekbones. Brooding, dark eyes.

She swallowed nervously, suddenly feeling giddy as a schoolgirl. "Come in before you turn into snowmen." Stepping back, she held the door open for them to enter.

Lucas was beaming proudly. "Andrea, this is my son, Dr. Shepler Wilde. Shep, Miss Andrea Dillon."

Andrea offered her hand. "Very nice meeting you."

Shep's hand around hers gave her an unexpected jolt. "Nice of you to have me over," he said without so much as a hint of a smile.

His coolness was so unexpected, Andrea flushed. Swiftly she withdrew her hand from his. "Give me your jackets, and I'll hang them in the closet."

Both men removed their jackets and handed them to her. "Come on into the living room, Lucas," she said, heading in that direction herself to hang the jackets in the small guest closet near the front door.

"Your tree is beautiful," Lucas said. "Isn't it nice, Shep?"

"Very nice," Shep agreed.

Closing the door of the closet, Andrea turned to her guests. "Please sit down. Dinner will be ready in about ten minutes. Just make yourself comfortable while I finish up." She had dinner wine chilling in the refrigerator, but no other spirits in the house. If Dr. Wilde enjoyed a before-dinner drink, she had nothing to offer him. He would have to content himself with a comfortable chair, a view of the tree and the lovely music on the CD player.

Smiling weakly, she hurriedly returned to the kitchen. Her heart was pounding. Good Lord, she thought, disgusted that she would be so physically affected just from meeting a man. Especially when he hadn't shown any signs of the same affliction with her.

But he was newly divorced and unhappy about it. What kind of person would he be if he could forget that sort of pain in the space of two minutes just because another woman had entered his life?

Placing her hands on the edge of the counter, she let her head drop forward. This was ridiculous. She had to calm her racing pulse and behave like an intelligent human being.

But no man she'd ever met had done to her what Shep Wilde had just from a handshake. She'd felt electricity throughout her entire body during those few seconds, and it wasn't disappearing as quickly as she would like it to. As she lifted her head to stare out at the falling snow, her eyes narrowed slightly. How could she have felt so much without him feeling something, too?

Oh, Lord, that was all she needed right now, to fall for a guy who viewed her as all but invisible.

Shaking her head, she began mashing potatoes.

Two

———

Lucas couldn't compliment her enough during dinner. Andrea thanked him nicely and pretended that everything she cooked turned out so well. In truth, she had barely known how to boil water when she arrived in Rocky Ford. Teaching herself to cook had been one of the activities she'd used to pass time while she waited for the right moment to approach Charlie. Lucas had eaten with her before, and her first efforts at putting a full meal on the table hadn't been all that great.

But he was a man with an appetite and had seemed to like whatever she'd served him. Today even she thought dinner was delicious. The turkey was moist, the gravy rich and smooth, and the side dishes perfect complements to the meat. Dessert was pumpkin or apple pie, but both Lucas and Shep declined when she offered it, declaring they were too full to eat another bite.

She believed Lucas wholeheartedly. He had filled his plate twice and had appeared to enjoy every mouthful. Shep, however, had eaten very little. He'd taken small portions and eaten them slowly, as though there was no hunger anywhere in his system and he was merely being polite.

"We'll have dessert later," Andrea said with more cheeriness than she felt. Shep Wilde had had her sitting on the edge of her chair throughout the meal, although he had certainly done or said nothing to cause such an unusual reaction. Lucas had chattered away a mile a minute, talking about the weather, Shep's long drive from California and Andrea's good cooking, and she had tried her level best to keep the conversational ball rolling. But even Shep's voice affected her—the few times he'd spoken during the meal—and looking directly into his dark eyes actually gave her goose bumps.

The two men were waiting for her direction, she realized. Rising, she smiled. "Why don't you make yourselves comfortable in the living room while I put away the food? I'll only be a few minutes."

Lucas pushed back his chair. "I'm going to help with these dishes, young woman. And don't try to argue me out of it. Shep, you go on into the living room and relax. Andrea and I will have everything shipshape in ten minutes."

Shep looked at Andrea standing there, awaiting her guests' decisions with an anticipatory expression, and felt a stirring in his groin. He'd felt the same thing the minute he'd set eyes on this woman and, in fact, all during the fine meal she had put on the table. When Lucas told him that he'd called the lady next door, and that she had said to bring him along to dinner, he had immediately gotten a mental picture of an older woman, someone around his father's age. He'd only agreed to come because Lucas had been so insistent. It had been a long time since he'd seen his father, and it was Christmas. Otherwise, he would have refused. His mood wasn't one for meeting new people, even his father's friends.

Then the door to Andrea's house had opened, and he'd felt that zap of awareness. Miss Andrea Dillon was young, beautiful, stunningly dressed and as sexy as any woman he'd ever seen. In fact, she was probably sexier, because sex was what he'd thought of all during dinner. Not that he'd arrived in Rocky Ford with any silly ideas about sex and women. Lord preserve him from another heartrending relationship. Natalie's desertion had all but destroyed him, and the last thing he wanted was another woman. In truth, he had wondered if he would *ever* want another woman.

But here was fate, or something, causing his traitorous body to respond to the first attractive woman he'd met in ages. It really was too much, and he sure as hell wasn't going to do anything about his ludicrous physical reactions to the sensuous Miss Dillon. It made him angry that he couldn't seem to eradicate those reactions, but he wasn't blaming Andrea and the anger was aimed at himself. After all, she couldn't help being beautiful, sultry and sexually intriguing. Nor was it her fault that his hormones were raging as though he were an adolescent ogling his first unclothed female breast.

Drawing in a long breath, he nodded and headed for the living room. Andrea left to help his father with the dishes.

In the living room, Shep sat in an easy chair from which he could look out the front window at the lazily falling snow. It was a pretty sight, but the Christmas music on the CD player was emotionally wrenching. Thoughts of the past few months deluged him: learning by accident that Natalie was seeing another man; confronting her with expectations of denial and hearing instead, "I want a divorce"; then the arguments; the pleas on his part; Natalie's rock-solid determination; his last-ditch effort to win her back by willingly signing a property settlement giving her everything she asked for; her departure for Mexico to get it over with quickly; and finally the day she returned home with divorce papers and told him to pack his personal possessions and get out of her house.

There was no hope left; it was truly over. He had moved into a hotel and tried to resume his life. But most of his patients were rich, spoiled people who spent a great deal of their time fighting old age, and he had found himself canceling appointments. The reason for his successful practice was a bitter pill to swallow. Natalie's father was a major producer in the movie industry. He had sent stars, directors and everyone else he knew that wanted a new nose, tummy tuck or some sort of surgical procedure, to Shep's office.

Shep had dreamed of a much different practice before meeting Natalie while he was still interning. He had wanted to limit his vocation to accident victims or people born with congenital defects, people who truly needed reconstructive surgery.

But he'd let himself be dazzled by the life-styles of the rich and famous, and had opened a fancy office in a fancy building and had started making incredible amounts of money from breast implants and face-lifts. For a man from a small town in Montana, it had all seemed like a dream—a gorgeous wife, famous friends and more money than he could spend.

It wasn't more than Natalie could spend, however. The truth was that he had worked his fanny off, having become addicted to those astonishing fees. But no matter how much money he put in the bank, it had a way of disappearing. With what Natalie had received in the divorce settlement, he found himself close to being broke. Disillusioned, unhappy with his work and broke. Yes, he could have geared up and built up his bank account. But nothing had held much meaning anymore.

A week ago he'd parceled out his remaining patients to other doctors, closed his fancy office, packed his car and headed for Montana. Not to burden Lucas with his personal problems, God forbid, but to give himself some breathing space. And maybe to find himself again, to figure out what he wanted to do with the rest of his life.

Staring almost hypnotically at the falling snow, he felt the emptiness within himself, the lack of purpose and ambition and the strangest urge to do nothing but watch snow fall or something equally mundane from this day forward. What had working hard gotten him? Why exert so much effort when this was the result?

He could hear Andrea and his father in the kitchen, moving about, talking to each other and laughing every so often. With a wall between him and Andrea, he could think of her as just another person. During dinner, he had not had that luxury. Her every movement had impacted his libido. Her eyes were especially beautiful, heavily lashed and that striking shade of green, and he doubted if her face and figure had ever been altered by a surgeon.

But there was something about her that didn't ring a hundred percent true. Take that comment Lucas had made about her being from California, for instance. Shep hadn't been contributing much to the conversation and had been feeling a little guilty about it—after all, he was a stranger she'd invited into her home and deserved some courtesy no matter how down in the dumps he felt—so he had pursued the topic his father had introduced. "What part of California?" he had asked Andrea. His eyes narrowed as he remembered how cleverly she had evaded a straight answer. And how she had immediately changed the subject.

Now, why would she avoid an innocuous discussion of her life before moving to Rocky Ford? And what had brought her to Montana in the first place? Did she have family here? If so, why wasn't she spending Christmas with them?

Yes indeed, there was something a little off kilter about Miss Dillon.

Shep sighed. Hell, she could have a scandalous or even a criminal past, and he wouldn't care.

He suddenly couldn't sit there any longer. Rising, he went to the closet for his jacket and put it on. Taking a pair of leather gloves from a pocket, he began working them onto his hands as he entered the kitchen.

"I'm going for a walk," he announced.

Andrea was loading the dishwasher, and Lucas was putting a covered dish into the refrigerator. They both became statue still and looked at him.

"Uh...sure," Lucas finally said. "Enjoy yourself, son."

"We'll have dessert and coffee when you get back," Andrea said.

He wanted to tell her not to wait for him, that he didn't know when he'd be back or even if he'd return to her house at all.

But he only nodded and walked out the back door.

Andrea and Lucas looked at each other. "He really is very unhappy, isn't he?" she said quietly.

"I'm afraid he is," Lucas said, sounding deeply concerned.

"Lucas, if you want to go after him, please don't feel as though you need to keep me company."

Lucas placed the dish in his hand on a refrigerator shelf and closed the door. "I think he wants to be alone, Andrea. He'll talk to me when he's ready."

"Well . . . I guess you know your own son."

"I used to," Lucas said in a saddened tone of voice.

Andrea began wiping down the counter. "He came to you, Lucas. In his time of trouble, he came home. That has to mean something."

Lucas's countenance brightened a little. "Yes, he did, didn't he?"

Andrea looked out the window above the sink. "It's snowing harder. Oh, it's lovely." But it was also freezing cold out there, and she couldn't help worrying about Shep Wilde walking around in such weather in an unhappy daze.

But he was a grown man and none of her business.

Briskly she turned to Lucas. "Everything's in order in here. Thank you very much for the help. Now, shall we retire to the living room? I'll build a fire in the fireplace, and we can either watch a movie or just sit and relax until Shep gets back."

They started for the living room. "How about if I build the fire and you pick out a movie?" Lucas said.

Andrea smiled. "If that's what you want, sure. What'll it be, a Western, a mystery or a romantic comedy?" She opened the cabinet that contained her collection of movies.

Lucas was already bending over to lay a fire. "Anything you choose is fine with me."

Andrea sighed inwardly. Lucas didn't care what movie she put in the VCR because of Shep out walking in the cold and snow.

Well, wasn't that where her mind would be, as well?

Today was not turning out at all the way she'd planned. But had any Christmas of her life been storybook perfect? Sighing again, she grabbed a movie without checking its title and inserted it in the VCR.

The best part of the next few hours was the fire crackling in the fireplace. Andrea didn't even attempt to concentrate on the movie, and twenty minutes into the film, Lucas was dozing. She looked at him with great affection. Men were such strange creatures. As worried as Lucas was about his son, he could still fall asleep in front of the TV.

She should be so lucky. Insomnia had been a problem ever since coming to Rocky Ford. When she was worried or upset, she simply couldn't sleep soundly, and rarely did she go to bed without something heavy on her mind. And she couldn't remember the last time she'd napped during the day.

The movie ended. Using the remote control, Andrea rewound it and then ejected it from the VCR. Getting up, she laid chunks of wood on the dying fire. It blazed again, and she sat on the hearth rug to watch the flames.

"I must have dozed off."

Turning to look at Lucas, she smiled. "You had a very nice nap."

"That was darned rude of me." Lucas got out of his chair and went to the window. "Any sign of Shep?"

"Your taking a nap was not rude, and no, I haven't seen Shep." Her sympathies were with Dr. Wilde. She had never gone through anything remotely similar to his divorce, but she was able to imagine how alone and lost one might feel over such an experience.

She got to her feet. "This is a good time to give you your present." Ignoring Lucas's startled expression, she went to the tree, reached way under it and came out with a gaily wrapped package.

"Andrea, you shouldn't have," Lucas said. "I didn't get you anything."

"And don't you dare be embarrassed by it." Andrea held out the package. "This is something I wanted to do and I didn't expect anything in return." She placed the gift in his hand. "Open it."

"This is really nice of you." In spite of her admonition to not be embarrassed, Lucas looked a little red in the face. But there was also a twinkling excitement in his eyes, making Andrea smile.

"Open it, Lucas," she repeated.

"Okay." Returning to his chair, he tore off the wrapping and removed the cover of a small box. "Well, look at this," he declared.

It was a soft, wool-blend maroon scarf, quite beautiful and much more expensive than what Andrea had planned on spending when she thought of buying him a Christmas gift. Running across it in a nondescript little shop with an eclectic assortment of merchandise had been a surprise, as Rocky Ford's stores normally didn't carry what she considered fashionable items of clothing. She would have bought it at any price. Lucas's best jacket, which he'd worn to her house today, was a dark gray wool, and she'd known at first sight that the scarf would be perfect with that jacket.

"How'd you know I needed a new scarf?" Lucas asked, holding it up and fingering the fabric. "Andrea, this is really nice. As soft as can be. Never could stand scratchy things around my neck."

"You like it, then?"

"Sure do."

"I'm glad. I thought it would go well with your gray jacket."

Lucas grinned impishly. "I'll look so smartly turned out, I'll probably have to fight off the ladies."

Andrea teased right back. "I'm sure you're already having to fight off the ladies."

Lucas chuckled. "Not anymore, honey." Carefully folding the scarf, he laid it in its box. "Well, I feel like a darned fool for not thinking to buy you something, but thank you. I appreciate your thoughtfulness."

"You're very welcome. I appreciate your friendship."

* * *

While this pleasant scene was unfolding in Andrea's house, Shep was pacing his father's home. He had walked in the heavy snowfall for about an hour, when he'd started feeling the cold, then bypassed Andrea's place in favor of Lucas's.

But he was feeling guilty about it. And besides, the house was so empty. Regardless of his personal upheaval, it was still Christmas, and it wasn't a good feeling to be alone on Christmas. Shep's guilt increased. How many Christmases had Lucas spent alone? Shep knew how badly he had neglected his father for years, and Lucas was just next door. He should be spending the day with him, wherever he was.

It finally got to him enough that he again donned his jacket and gloves and plowed through the snow to Andrea's back door. Swearing that he was going to be friendlier than before—his problems were neither Lucas's nor Andrea's fault, and they shouldn't have to endure his foul moods—he knocked.

Lucas's face brightened. "That must be Shep."

"Must be," Andrea agreed. "I'll go let him in." It felt as though her heart were doing flips as she hurried through the house to the kitchen door. It was incredibly exciting to be so dizzily attracted to a man, even if she wished he weren't Shep Wilde and newly divorced.

She opened the door with a smile, expecting to see him covered in snow and half-frozen. But he was neither; rather, appearing as though he had just come from next door as he had earlier today.

She knew he had gone to Lucas's home instead of taking that walk. He really wasn't a very nice person, was he? Coming up with a lie like that to get away from her and his father? She knew he'd been bored and impatient with the day's quiet activity, but for his father's sake it certainly wouldn't have killed him to pretend to enjoy himself.

Her expression became frosty. "Come in."

Then the biggest surprise of the day thus far occurred. Shep smiled. Not just smiled, but smiled *at her!* Andrea suddenly couldn't breathe, and the frost in her expression melted into a puddle of totally female emotions. "*Do* come in," she repeated huskily, this time sounding sincerely welcoming.

"Thank you."

Shep stepped inside and Andrea shut the door. My Lord, she thought. If his smile could make her breathless, what would a kiss do to her?

"Shep?"

Lucas was calling from the living room.

"I'm here, Dad." Removing his jacket, Shep looked at Andrea. "I can hang it up myself, if it's all right with you."

Anything you want to do is all right with me. "Yes, of course. Go right ahead."

They paraded into the living room. Shep spotted the fire. "That looks great." He hung his jacket in the closet and immediately went over to the fireplace.

"You were out there a long time, son," Lucas said. "You must be cold clear to the center of your bones."

Shep turned around and stood with his backside to the fire. "I wasn't walking all the time I was gone, Dad. I went home for a while."

So, Andrea thought, inordinately pleased. He wasn't a liar, after all. And he probably hadn't been trying to avoid her and Lucas; he'd merely needed to be alone. Poor guy. Since he was so broken up over it, the divorce must not have been his idea.

"Well," Andrea said brightly. "Is anyone hungry?"

"I could use a turkey sandwich," Shep said, giving her another of those dazzling smiles.

"I can always eat," Lucas said with a chuckle.

"Great. I'll put everything on the table. It'll only take a few minutes." Breathless again, Andrea sped to the kitchen. The day had taken a marvelous turn, simply because Shep Wilde was smiling instead of scowling. His hike in the snow had worked some sort of miracle. Or maybe he was finally glad to be home for Christmas.

Or maybe, just maybe, he had come to grips with liking her. With finding another woman attractive so soon after his divorce. Hadn't she noticed his brooding glances at the dinner table?

Hastily she sliced turkey and set the table, all the while thinking about Shep. Okay, she admitted, so she had it bad for him, and it could be very dangerous business. But what if he felt the same about her? Would a rebound romance *be* dangerous if both parties felt the same overwhelming emotions for each other?

"Don't put the cart before the horse," she muttered under her breath in a sudden burst of common sense. A few smiles were hardly an admission of attraction. And what was sadder than a person—man or woman—falling for someone who didn't reciprocate? She really must watch her step around Shep, especially when Lucas was looking on. Appearing foolish or pathetic in Lucas's eyes would be unbearable. No, she could never let that happen.

Squaring her shoulders, she went to the doorway between kitchen and living room. "Everything's ready," she said with an inviting smile. "Come and eat."

Andrea enjoyed listening to Lucas and Shep talk about old friends in Rocky Ford while they ate. It occurred to her that Shep could be asking about this person or that just to make conversation, but she still read it as a good sign. At least he was trying, which was a lot more than he'd done before.

Most of the people mentioned were strangers to Andrea, but her ears pricked up and her pulse began racing when Shep asked, "And how are the Fanons doing?"

Lucas grinned. "That's right. I'd forgotten you were sweet on Lola Fanon for a while."

Shep grinned, too. "In high school, Dad. A very long time ago. Anyhow, do they still live around here?"

"Sure do. Charlie lives in the same house he always did, as a matter of fact. You know about his coffee shop, don't you?"

"You took me there the last time I was home," Shep reminded. "About eight years ago," he added quietly.

Andrea saw a glint of remorse in Shep's eyes. Obviously, he was regretting his long absence, probably feeling guilty over neglecting his father for eight long years.

Well, he should feel guilty, she thought to herself rather fiercely. If she ever connected with her father, she would never neglect him.

She cleared her throat. "I've run across the Fanon name several times. What kind of man is Charlie?"

Lucas answered. "Real nice guy, Andrea. I doubt if there's anyone in Rocky Ford who doesn't like him. If they've met him, of course."

"What about the rest of the family?" Shep asked. "Does Ron still live here?"

"Ron's dead, Shep," Lucas said gently.

"Dead! What happened?" Shep inquired, obviously stunned.

"He died while in the military. I don't know the particulars, but Charlie went to Germany—that's where Ron was stationed—and brought his body back here for burial. Brought his wife and little boy with him, too. Candace— that was Ron's wife—remarried about a month ago. Maybe a little longer."

Shep fell silent for a few moments, then inquired quietly, "And Serena? Lola?"

"They're both married and living in the area. Serena's a lawyer with an office in the Ridgeport Building. Her husband, Travis Holden, owns a string of car lots all over Montana. Lola married Duke Sheridan and they, of course, live on the Sheridan Ranch. I'm sure you remember the Sheridans."

Lucas's knowledge of the Fanon family surprised Andrea, though she didn't let on. But she was learning more about life in a small town all the time. Even if people weren't close friends, they seemed to know what everyone else was doing. This was new to her. Sandra had always shied away from small communities, preferring cities and elegant neighborhoods where people were rather standoffish. Actually, Andrea had to admire her mother. While her life-style hadn't been wonderful for her daughter, she had certainly gotten around, and however often they had moved, it had never taken Sandra very long to insinuate herself into a new neighborhood and become a part of it, however reserved and aloof the residents were.

And she'd been so beautiful. So stylish, so chic. Small wonder she'd attracted men by the droves.

Andrea sighed. While she'd obviously inherited some of her mother's best physical features, she certainly hadn't gotten much of her intrepidness. Nothing had ever daunted Sandra as facing Charlie Fanon daunted Andrea.

Around six, Lucas said it was time they went home. Andrea hated to see them go, but she put on a smile and saw them to the door. Just before leaving, Shep shook her hand again. "Thank you for today, Andrea. You're a gracious hostess."

Looking into his dark eyes, she again felt that constrictive band around her chest. If she counted every man she'd met in her whole life, Shep Wilde was the most handsome. And no other man had *ever* caused such volcanic reactions in her system, not even those she had liked and dated.

Lucas broke up the handshake by holding up the box he was carrying. "Thanks again for the gift, Andrea."

She saw Shep look at the box, but he said nothing about it. Father and son walked out the door and called goodnights. It was dark outside and still snowing. The biting cold had Andrea quickly closing the door behind them.

Then, sighing, she went to the living room and added wood to the fire. It was too quiet now, and she put another CD into the player. Seated in her favorite chair, she laid her head back and thought about the day. Overall, it had been a good Christmas, she decided.

Far better than many she remembered.

Shep and Lucas hurried into the house. It wasn't a night to linger outdoors, and Lucas's modest home was warm and cozy. After hanging up their jackets, they sat in the living room. Shep could tell that his father wanted to ask questions, and he decided to make it easy for Lucas by telling him everything without prompting.

"She left me for another man," he said bluntly.

Lucas looked stunned and incredulous. "Shep, are you sure?"

Shep gave a sharp little laugh, one with no humor in it whatsoever. "I'm sure. A friend told me she was seeing someone—using every subtlety in the book to say it without actually saying it. I called him a liar, backtracked and said he must be mistaken and then talked to Natalie that night, expecting denials and anger that anyone would intimate such a thing about her." Shep's expression became bitter. "She said it was true and asked for a divorce."

Lucas was still stunned. "But, son, a woman who is happy and contented with her marriage doesn't go looking for another man."

Shep's lips twisted cynically. "Maybe they don't in Rocky Ford, but southern California isn't Rocky Ford, Montana, Dad."

"Are you telling me you never had a clue that something was wrong before your friend mentioned it? Incidentally, I don't have a lot of respect for someone who's supposedly a friend carrying tales like that."

"If there were clues, I never picked up on them," Shep said. "As for Jeff talking about Natalie like that, wasn't he trying to do me a favor? It was damned hard for him to broach the subject, and he risked our friendship to let me know what was going on. I don't hold anything against Jeff, Dad. It would have been worse for him to know about it and not say anything."

Lucas shook his head sadly. "Don't see how it could have been any worse, Shep. All this time, I believed your marriage was solid as a rock and that both you and Natalie were happy. Now, here you are, divorced and miserable. You two should have had kids."

"So we could have fought over their custody? Kids don't hold a marriage together, Dad. Only love does that. Apparently, Natalie didn't love me."

"She did at first, didn't she?"

"I thought so," Shep said, letting his bitterness show again.

"Well, at least you have your practice," Lucas said, obviously assuming Shep would find comfort in his work.

Shep wasn't ready to talk about that. He didn't know what he was going to do about his career. He'd spent so many years in getting an education, and they'd been hard years. Lucas had helped out financially with what he could afford, but a medical education, especially when it included a specialty, was extremely costly. Those were years of doing without, of barely getting by, years when he'd done very little beyond studying, working at whatever job he could find to earn a few extra bucks and living without enough sleep.

He'd been interning at Los Angeles General Hospital, on the very last leg of his education, when he met Natalie Draper.

Her world had dazzled him. *She* had dazzled him. Beautiful, vivacious and without a care in the world, Natalie had had hordes of friends, most of whom had seemingly existed for one reason—the next party, whether it be a fundraiser, the opening of one more elegant or campy restaurant, or film-industry events, such as the Academy Awards gala. Always dressed in designer clothing, Natalie missed nothing that Hollywood and its icons had had to offer.

It had taken Shep a while to believe that a fashionable, wealthy, gorgeous young woman like Natalie Draper would want him. He'd definitely been head over heels for her, but a penniless intern was so far from her realm of existence, it had been a massive shock to finally realize that she was truly serious about him.

She'd taken him home to meet Daddy—and Daddy's third wife. Brad Draper hadn't been nearly as charmed as Natalie was by an almost doctor with a yet unknown future. But Shep still to this day had to hand it to Brad; he'd put aside his own misgivings and eventually welcomed him into the family.

Ten years, Shep thought with another onslaught of bitterness. Ten years down the drain. He was back to square one, or damned near. No wife, no practice and very little money weren't exactly consoling, especially when he hadn't seen it coming.

What kind of fool had he been?

He suddenly realized that Lucas was watching him with an uneasy expression. But why wouldn't his dad be uneasy? He hadn't given him any kind of answer to his comment about him at least having his medical practice, had he?

Well, he had none to give. When he himself knew what was coming next, he'd be glad to inform Lucas about it. Getting to his feet, he stretched and yawned. "I'm beat, Dad. I'm going to hit the sack."

Lucas frowned. "Well, sure, son. Go right ahead." Before Shep made it out of the room, he added, "What do you think of my next-door neighbor?"

"Andrea's a very nice person," Shep said evenly, omitting deliberately so much as a hint of the libidinous urges she had aroused in him all day. "Good night, Dad. See you in the morning."

"Good night, Shep. Sleep well."

Three

———

Andrea slept well, but she awoke at 8:00 a.m. with prickly feelings of dissatisfaction. It had happened before in Rocky Ford, and she always blamed the sensation on impatience with herself over forever delaying that meeting with Charlie Fanon.

This morning, she wasn't thinking of Charlie. The image in her mind's eye was most definitely that of Shep Wilde. Too handsome, she told herself, even while tingling all over because he *was* so handsome. But Shep wasn't the reason for the uneasiness she felt, either.

It took only a few minutes to come up with a logical diagnosis of the problem: there was no reason to get up. She could stay in bed for the rest of her life, and who would care? This doing nothing, or almost nothing, had to stop. It seemed she had made an unconscious decision to live in Rocky Ford, whether or not she ever introduced herself to Charlie, so it was time to start living.

And she knew precisely where the starting line was, too.

Throwing back the covers, she got up and padded bare-foot to the kitchen to make a pot of coffee. A glance out the window to her backyard had her grimacing. Before she could put her plan in motion, before she could go any-where, for that matter, she had to shovel the driveway again. It wasn't snowing this morning, but there were at least six inches on the ground.

Returning to her bedroom, she dressed in warm clothing and lined boots. Heading for her small garage and the snow shovel, she stopped and blinked in surprise. Her driveway had already been shoveled!

Lucas, bless his heart, must have done it before she was even awake. What a sweetheart.

She would thank him later on today, she thought as she returned to the house. After she had called on Kathleen Osterman, the owner and publisher of the *Rocky Ford News*. Yes, she was going to ask Ms. Osterman about a job. If there was nothing available at the newspaper, she would look elsewhere, but her first choice was definitely the local paper.

After coffee, toast and orange juice in the kitchen, she showered, did her hair and makeup and dressed in an at-tractive gray wool pantsuit. Under the jacket was a plain black sweater with a high neck. Her jewelry was gold ear-rings, a gold-and-black onyx pin on the lapel of her jacket and her gold watch. Stepping into her best black leather boots, she checked her appearance in the full-length mir-ror on her closet door. Satisfied with her reflection, she donned a long, dark gray overcoat, pulled on black leather gloves, slung her black leather bag over her shoulder and left the house for the garage.

Raising the door of the garage, she got into her car and started the engine. Giving it time to warm up, she thought of how differently one lived where winter was a true sea-son. Cars needed extra antifreeze and snow tires, and peo-ple needed a wardrobe of warm clothing. She had never owned a winter coat before this year, for instance. Fash-ionable ski suits, of course, but nothing like what she was wearing today. She had found some of her cold-weather clothes in Rocky Ford, and some she had purchased from catalogs. Her overcoat, for example, had been purchased from an exclusive and very expensive house of fashion through their catalog.

When the heater was blowing warm air, she quit her meandering thoughts and backed out of the driveway to the street. Granted, there were butterflies in her tummy over this unannounced visit to Ms. Osterman, but they were flutters of excitement. Just the thought of working again, having something to do and somewhere to go, was exhilarating. She should have looked for a job long before this.

Andrea drove to the newspaper office, found a parking space and walked into the one-story building. She loved it at once, from its unique smell of newsprint to its air of productivity. It wasn't large and it wasn't noisy, but newspapers were created here. She would love to be a part of it.

The front of the building was one large room. Several doors drew her attention; one had to lead to the pressroom. Two women sat at desks, one of whom was talking on the phone. The other looked up.

"May I help you?"

Andrea smiled. "I'd like to speak to Kathleen Osterman. Is she in?"

"Do you have an appointment?"

"Is an appointment necessary?"

"No, but I thought she might be expecting you."

"She isn't, but I really would like to see her."

"I'll check with her. What's your name?"

"Andrea Dillon."

The woman dialed a number on her phone. "Kathleen, there's an Andrea Dillon out here who would like to speak to you. Do you have time to see her now?" After a beat, the woman said, "No, she didn't say what it was about. Should I ask her?" There was another pause, then she said, "Fine, I'll send her back." She put down the phone and looked at Andrea. "She'll see you. It's the door on the left. Just go on in."

The woman had pointed to the back of the room. "Thank you." Andrea rounded a short counter and crossed to Ms. Osterman's office door. But she couldn't just walk in, regardless of the instructions she'd received.

Drawing a breath, she knocked.

"Come in" came from the other side of the door. Though deep, gravelly and rather strident, it was unquestionably a female voice.

Andrea took another quick breath and opened the door. Her initial impression was of clutter. Papers, books and file folders were piled on anything that would hold them. Her gaze moved to the woman behind an enormous desk. "Ms. Osterman?"

"Ms. Dillon?" Kathleen sounded amused over their greeting. "Any relation to the Dillons who live on Green Street?" She gestured to the chair at the front of her desk. "Come in and have a seat."

"Thank you." Andrea shut the door and went to the chair. Settling herself, she smiled. "To answer your question, no, I'm not related to any Dillons in the area."

"Really." Kathleen sat back and blatantly sized up her visitor.

Andrea was doing a little sizing up herself. Kathleen Osterman was an extremely attractive woman, in her middle fifties, she estimated. Her clothing—a pair of taupe slacks and matching sweater—looked expensive. So did the cut of her short blond hair, her makeup and her jewelry. Several rings with large diamonds adorned her long, thin fingers. Her face was more striking than pretty, and her eyes—a deep, dark blue—looked hard as marbles.

This lady was no cream puff, Andrea decided.

"So, what can I do for you, Miss Dillon?" Kathleen asked, sounding blunt, businesslike and to the point.

"I'm looking for a job, Ms. Osterman."

Kathleen cocked an eyebrow. "And you think I have an opening?"

"Do you?"

"Do *you* know anything about the newspaper business?"

"Not as much as I would like to know," Andrea said. She was getting too warm and she slid her arms from her overcoat and let it fall back against the chair. "I worked for the *Los Angeles Times* for almost a year, but I have to be truthful. I was more of a secretary and a gofer than anything else. I want to be a reporter, Ms. Osterman. I'm a good writer, although the only paper that ever published anything of mine was the student gazette at the college I attended. I have clippings of my articles in my purse, if you'd care to see them. Incidentally, I majored in journalism," she added as a final note. "And graduated with honors."

"Back up a minute. You worked for the *Times* for almost a year? If your heart's so set on journalism, why did you leave the *Times?* You had your foot in the door of one of the most widely read papers in the country. If you're as good a writer as you claim, eventually you would have worked your way into reporting. I think an explanation is in order, Miss Dillon."

Andrea maintained an impassive expression, although her heart had started beating faster than normal. She couldn't be honest and she didn't want to lie, but there was no way to avoid giving this woman some sort of explanation.

"My mother passed away last February. Her estate demanded my full attention. I would have stayed at the *Times* if not for that." It was as close to the truth as she could get.

"Your mother's estate brought you to Rocky Ford?" Kathleen looked skeptical.

"In a roundabout way, yes. Things have settled down now, and I'd like to go back to work." Andrea smiled. "But something happened during my stay in Rocky Ford, something I certainly didn't expect when I came here. I've grown to love Montana and this little town. The thought of returning to L.A. is not at all appealing."

Still appearing skeptical, Kathleen picked up a cup and drank from it. "Coffee," she said. "Would you like some?"

"No, thank you."

Kathleen set down her cup. "Let me tell you how it is, Miss Dillon. My paper comes out only three times a week, and—"

"I know," Andrea murmured. "I've bought and read it since the day I came to Rocky Ford."

"Then you also know that we pick up only the most urgent national and international news from the wire services, and that most of the paper is dedicated to reporting events that would only be of interest to the locals."

Andrea nodded. "I think it's a wonderful format for a small-town paper. Those residents interested in more-detailed stories of world events can find them in any number of other newspapers."

Kathleen's expression became slightly sarcastic. "So glad you approve."

Andrea flushed. "I'm sorry if I sounded patronizing. I merely intended to convey my own enjoyment of reading your publication." Working for Kathleen Osterman would not be easy. But then, there was probably no reason to worry about it. Ms. Osterman wasn't exactly elated over this interview.

"Getting back to how my organization functions, I'm the only reporter on the payroll, Miss Dillon."

Startled, Andrea blinked. "You write every article yourself?"

"I didn't say that. I said I'm the only full-time, salaried reporter. I have three employees. You saw two of them on your way in. Grace Mulroy handles the classifieds, without which we wouldn't stay in business for long. The woman who sent you to my office is a jack-of-all-trades, secretary, receptionist, delivery person, et cetera, et cetera. You name it, Sally does it. My third employee is the pressman. Now, besides those three very essential people, I hire a photographer when necessary and buy free-lance articles. Anyone can bring something in. If I think it's good enough, it goes in the paper. I pay sixty-five cents a line. Can you live on sixty-five cents a line, Miss Dillon? Assuming your articles are published, of course."

"Money isn't an issue," Andrea said quietly, disliking this topic immensely. It really was no one else's business that she had enough money to live very comfortably for the rest of her life. "But I need something to do. Naturally, your newspaper was the first thing I thought of when I came to that realization. What kind of articles are we talking about?"

Kathleen shrugged. "Weddings, funerals, any sort of social function, accidents. Anything, actually. Let me warn you. If you're thinking of free-lancing, you'll have lots of competition. Especially with weddings and events of that nature."

"I understand." Andrea began working her arms back into her coat. "Well, thank you for seeing me."

"You're disappointed."

"I won't lie about it, Ms. Osterman. I came here hoping for a full-time job."

Kathleen got up from her chair. "You want to know something, Miss Dillon? I have a feeling that the most intriguing story you could write for this paper would be about yourself."

Andrea rose. Kathleen definitely had a nose for news. It was blatantly obvious she wasn't satisfied with Andrea's explanation of why she was living in Rocky Ford.

Andrea forced a laugh, as though Kathleen's curiosity was funny and certainly of no consequence. Then she picked up her purse. "Again, thank you for your time."

"Will we meet again, Miss Dillon?" Kathleen's agate eyes bored into Andrea.

"You're asking if I plan to free-lance. I don't know, Ms. Osterman. I'm going to think about it. Goodbye."

Andrea felt Kathleen's hard blue eyes on her back all the way to the front door of the building. Apparently, the publisher had left her office to watch her departure, probably with a rapidly working mind just teeming with all sorts of questions.

Well, Kathleen had a right to her curiosity, just as *she* had a right to her disappointment. Heading for her car, she got in and drove away.

Instead of going home, however, she made several turns until she came to Foxworth Street. Then, as she'd done a hundred times in the past seven months, she slowly cruised by Charlie's Place. It always looked the same and it always affected her emotionally. Inside that sprawling structure was her father. Physically, it would be so simple to park and enter Charlie's coffee shop. It was at that point that her imagination usually failed her.

This morning was slightly different, though. Lucas pronouncing Charlie Fanon a nice guy yesterday was fresh fodder for thought. Nice guys didn't turn their backs on their offspring, did they?

But he *had* turned his back on her, before she was even born.

That was the wall she kept hurling herself at and never quite managed to scale. If only her mother would have talked about Charlie. Sandra could have told her so much.

Andrea's heart hardened a little. Sandra hadn't been fair with her, not fair at all.

Disappointed with her talk with Kathleen and despondent about Charlie again, Andrea pointed her car toward home.

That afternoon, Andrea knocked on Lucas's door. When he opened it, she put a large covered pan in his hands. "I meant to give you this last night, Lucas. It's turkey and pie. There's no way I would be able to eat all the leftovers."

Lucas beamed. "Thank you. Would you like to come in?"

Still unnerved over the morning's depressing events, Andrea sighed. "No, but thank you. I'm going to run now." She'd thrown on a sweater for the short hike from her house to Lucas's, and was feeling the cold. She started to go, then remembered something. "Oh, by the way, thanks for shoveling my driveway again."

"You're welcome, honey, but I didn't do it. Shep did."

"Shep did?"

"He was up early and did mine before first light. When I got up, he was pacing like a caged tiger. I told him if he wanted some more exercise to go next door and do yours."

"Well," Andrea said, surprised and unable to conceal it. In a few seconds, she had gathered her wits enough to add, "Tell him thanks for me, okay? See you later, Lucas." Shivering, she dashed home.

In the kitchen, she stood over the furnace vent to warm up. It was a gray day and much too cold to be running around outside in only a sweater. She hadn't caught a cold or a flu bug yet this winter, though both were certainly going around, and getting herself chilled was a foolish risk.

But she'd wanted to take that food over to Lucas and simply hadn't thought beyond that. More accurately, she'd been preoccupied, mostly thinking of her chat with Kathleen and wishing she could write something so brilliant, it would knock Ms. Osterman's costly boots right off of her undoubtedly elegantly pedicured feet.

The problem, of course, was a topic to write about. Since she knew so few people in Rocky Ford, weddings and other social events weren't a consideration. Besides, she wasn't even a tiny bit interested in writing that sort of piece, although if Kathleen had deigned to hire her as a full-time reporter, she would have written anything.

Free-lancing was a whole other ball game. Of course, she could chuck the whole idea and seek some other kind of work. Deep down, though, she wanted to prove something to Kathleen Osterman. Prove herself, probably. Some people brought that urge out in others, and, in Andrea's opinion, Kathleen was definitely in that category—hard as nails, exceedingly sure of herself and not particularly sympathetic toward would-be journalists.

Biting on her bottom lip and frowning, Andrea left the hot-air vent and went into the living room. She seemed to be approaching a truth about herself, and it wasn't very comforting. Her self-esteem was at an all-time low. A voice in the back of her head told her to forget Charlie Fanon, pack her things and go to a city where she could find the kind of job that would renew her self-worth. She'd been proud to have secured a job at the *Times,* for instance, and she longed to feel worthwhile again. What was she now, other than a lonely, rather pathetic woman with no purpose whatsoever? In effect, her life was in limbo. It had been in limbo since the day she drove into Rocky Ford, only it had taken her a long time to realize it.

Well, she realized it now.

So... what was she going to do about it?

The word *limbo* was also in Shep's thoughts, almost at the same time Andrea had been thinking it, strangely enough. Driving around town with the excuse of seeing old friends—he never stopped once to say hello to anyone—he wondered if coming home hadn't been a mistake.

And yet, if he hadn't come here, where would he have gone? He was certain of only one thing: he was not going back to Los Angeles.

So... where did that leave him?

The days between Christmas and New Year's clicked off. Andrea racked her brain for something to write about that hadn't been done a dozen times before, and Shep wandered every highway and back road in the county, regardless of the weather.

They didn't run into each other even once.

On New Year's Eve day, Andrea prepared herself for a solitary evening. Memories of getting ready for New Year's Eve parties in past years haunted her as she fixed snacks to eat while she watched other people bring in the New Year on television. One year, she remembered, she'd worn a short, brilliant green dress covered in sequins. She'd done her hair in a mass of small curls, and she had looked beautiful, carefree and happy. Hale had taken her to a crowded, noisy party, and they had danced and drunk champagne and laughed until three in the morning.

What a difference in comparison to tonight, she thought grimly. Around nine, she showered, pulled on a pair of gray sweats, ran a comb through her damp hair and settled down in front of the TV.

She sat there for an hour, but the merriment on the screen barely registered. What was Hale doing tonight? For certain, he wasn't sitting alone in his apartment, getting fat on cream-cheese-and-salmon canapés.

Maybe she should call him and wish him a happy New Year. Yes, why not? Why in heck not?

Getting up, she went to the phone and dialed his number from memory. She got his answering machine. "This is Hale. I might be home, but if I am, I'm *verrry* busy." There was a lascivious laugh. "Leave your name and number, and I'll return your call at my first available moment."

Andrea had always hated that message. But Hale considered himself a Hollywood stud and wanted everyone to think that if he wasn't out whooping it up or working in a movie, he was in bed with a woman. Once she'd gotten to know him, she'd realized he was almost always on stage, whether there was a camera present or not, and that beneath his tough-guy facade, he was really pretty normal.

And likable. He had an off-the-wall sense of humor that made her laugh. The one thing he hadn't done was lure her into bed. She liked Hale a lot, but not in a sexual way. He'd never quite understood that, but apparently he liked her, too, because he had kept asking her out.

"Hale, this is Andrea. I'm calling from Montana to wish you a happy New Year. Should have known you wouldn't be home. I have an unlisted number, but if you get the urge to call me back, it's 555-7707. Happy New Year, old friend."

Sighing, she put down the phone. If she played certain songs on her CD player, she would probably blubber like a baby.

So it was either television or bed.

No, she was going to see in the New Year if it killed her. Stubbornly she plopped herself back into her chair and picked a piece of peanut-butter-filled celery from her tray of goodies.

She was about to bite into it when someone knocked on her kitchen door. A frisson of fear went up her spine. *No one* knocked on her door at this time of night. Or they never had before. Rocky Ford residents went to bed with the birds, and she didn't really know any of them other than Lucas, anyway.

Maybe it *was* Lucas, she thought then, just dropping in to wish her a happy New Year. Gathering her courage, telling herself to not be such a baby, disgusted that her first reaction would be fear over someone knocking on her door, she got up and went to the kitchen.

But she wasn't so brave that she didn't call out, "Who is it?"

"Shep Wilde."

Her jaw dropped. Shep was here? Why?

"Oh, damn," she whispered, shaken that he would see her without makeup and her hair just hanging limply.

"Andrea?"

Bracing herself for the inevitable, she opened the door. "Hi." Naturally, he looked spectacular. That black leather jacket made his shoulders appear to be three feet wide. Then she noticed the bottle he was carrying and that he was smiling.

"Dad already went to bed," he said. "I saw your lights. How about bringing in the New Year with me? I've got some pretty good champagne here." He held up the bottle. "If you like champagne, that is."

"I . . . yes, of course. Come in." He was at her house to see in the New Year. And he was positively gorgeous. Her heart was suddenly singing. "I should have thought of inviting you and Lucas over, but . . ." What was her *but?*

Oh, to heck with it, she thought, smiling glowingly at Shep and holding the door open for him to come in. Arctic air flowed in with him, and she quickly shut the door again. "It's below zero tonight."

"About ten below, according to the thermometer on the post outside Dad's back door."

"Come into the living room. Oh, would you like the champagne put in the refrigerator?"

"I'd like it put in a couple of glasses."

"You don't want to save it for midnight?"

"It's a big bottle. There'll be enough left to toast the New Year."

"I'm going to excuse myself for a few minutes." She couldn't bear looking so colorless and plain, not when she was going to drink champagne with Shep Wilde. "Make yourself to home. I won't be long."

Shep knew that she was going to put on some makeup. He wished he knew her well enough to tell her she looked great just as she was.

But he'd come here on impulse, without the slightest ulterior motive, and he didn't want to do or say anything that would give her the wrong idea. Lucas's normal bedtime was 9:00 p.m. Tonight he'd tried very hard to stay alert and keep Shep company until midnight, but he'd fallen asleep in his chair and snored until Shep had awakened him and told him to go on to bed.

Then he'd sat there by himself until the edginess in his system took over, at which time he'd left his chair and started that infernal pacing he'd been doing much too often. It was as though he couldn't sit still for more than a few minutes anymore, especially when he was alone.

He had just happened to glance at a window and saw dim lights outside. Going closer to the glass, he'd peered through it; the lights were in Andrea's house.

He'd sucked in a breath, wondering if she was alone or had company.

It was easy to find out. Going outside, he'd walked to the fence and taken a look at her driveway. No vehicles meant no guests in this part of town.

Hurrying back inside—it was cold enough to freeze a man in midstride—he'd put on his jacket, taken the bottle of champagne that he'd bought for tonight from the refrigerator and left through the back door without further debate on the matter. Either she would welcome him or she wouldn't; it was as simple as that, and neither option would affect him all that much.

Of course, he *was* hoping during the hike to her door that she would see in the New Year with him. It was his own fault that he wasn't with old friends tonight. He'd been in town a week and hadn't contacted anyone. The thought of explaining why he was in Montana without his wife, and seeing sympathy or pity on anyone's face, made his skin crawl.

Andrea was a new friend or, at least, a new acquaintance. He wouldn't have to explain anything to her.

Locating two glasses in a cabinet, he opened the bottle. The cork popped and the champagne bubbled. Quickly he let the overflow spill into one of the glasses. Taking a swallow from the glass, he nodded; it was indeed good champagne. Filling the second glass, he brought them to the living room.

There was a fire in the fireplace and a tray of delicious-looking snacks on a table next to a chair. He helped himself to a cracker with cheese spread on it. The TV was on. Andrea had told him to make himself to home, so he turned down the volume on the television set and thumbed through her CDs until he found one he liked, which he inserted into the player.

Then, with his glass of champagne—he had placed the second one near the tray—he sat down. This was pleasant, he decided—a crackling fire, good music, snacks and cold champagne were a whole lot better than him sitting alone in his dad's house on New Year's Eve. In fact, he felt emotionally calmer and more physically relaxed than he had in months.

Stretching his legs out in front of him toward the fire, he sipped from his glass. Champagne wasn't his favorite drink—in truth, he wasn't particularly fond of alcoholic beverages of any kind—but it tasted good tonight. Eyeing Andrea's glass on the table with the tray, thinking her champagne would go flat if left standing like that for long, he wondered what was keeping her.

He frowned then. She wasn't going all out for him, was she? He could understand a woman wanting to slap on a little lipstick because of an unexpected guest, but primping for twenty, thirty minutes was another matter entirely.

Primping was exactly what Andrea was doing. Breathlessly trying to hurry. Worrying about what to put on. Excitedly thinking of Shep Wilde in her house.

Finally she was ready. Taking one last look in the mirror, she hastily assessed herself. Her long skirt and top, simply designed but in a stunning, ripe-cantaloupe color, was not subzero garb, but it was extremely flattering. Nervously running her hands down her hips, she took a deep breath and left her bedroom.

Her flat pumps made very little sound as she traversed the short hall to the living room. In the doorway, she stopped and looked at Shep, who was staring at the fire.

This was only the second time she had seen this man, and she knew in her heart that he could become very important to her. He must have some of the same feelings, or he wouldn't be here tonight of all nights, would he? This was a special holiday for most people, one that they spent with people they cared about. Shep would not be here if he thought of her as only a friend of his father's.

How incredibly thrilling. Not once since coming to Rocky Ford had she thought of romance, or lamented the lack thereof. But she was thinking of it now. It seemed to be pumping through her veins, saturating her system, making her feel warmly female and sensual.

Or something was.

What was it, if not romance?

Just looking at Shep was a pleasure of monumental proportions, but what was he thinking of so intently that he was unaware of her standing in the doorway?

Could it be her?

Smiling, she walked into the room. "Sorry I took so long."

Four

Shep looked at her, then got to his feet. "No problem," he told her, although it was a lie. She had suddenly become a very prominent problem. He had forgotten—or simply hadn't thought about it all week—how strongly she had affected him on Christmas. Even when she'd opened the door tonight, he hadn't felt any particular reaction.

But he felt one now. She was beautiful. Her dress was a knockout, and she'd drawn her hair into a loose knot on top of her head, with wispy curls and strands floating around her face and nape. She'd done a lot more than powder her nose and dab on some lipstick; her makeup was perfect.

Obviously, she had gone to so much trouble for him. Maybe she wanted something from him tonight and was saying so with her moistened, melon-colored lips and cosmetically enhanced gray green eyes. Wouldn't he be a damned fool to forgo the pleasure her stunning appearance promised?

On the other hand, an intimate relationship with a woman who might read more into it than he intended would hardly be wise. And she did live right next door.

All that ambiguity raced through Shep's mind so fast, Andrea wasn't even aware of a pause. Spotting the glass of champagne on the table with the snacks, she walked over and picked it up. "This must be mine."

Shep cleared his throat. "It is."

Andrea held up her glass. "Well . . . cheers."

Shep raised his glass. "Cheers."

They each took a swallow.

"Please sit down," Andrea said, sinking into her chair. The music registered. "I see you like rhythm and blues."

"You have a nice collection of CDs." Shep resumed his seat.

"A rather eclectic collection, actually."

"Yes, I noticed some Mozart and Chopin, and several country-music disks."

Andrea's smile contained amused self-indulgence. "I can't make up my mind which kind of music I like best." She took another swallow from her glass. "This is very good champagne."

"I was worried that I'd poured yours too soon. Didn't want it going flat before you drank it."

"It's not at all flat. Well, this is nice. I never dreamed someone would drop in tonight." She lifted her chin a little, looked directly into Shep's eyes and added in a soft and sexy voice, "Especially you."

His pulse picked up speed. That was a challenging comment if he'd ever heard one. He'd been right about her dressing up for him. The tingling in his groin raced up his spine.

"Why especially me?" His smile was deliberately light and without any challenges of his own. As exciting as Andrea was, he knew he would regret anything beyond friendship with her.

Andrea smiled in return, but it was *not* light, nor was it teasing. She had never liked a man more, nor had she ever been so physically attracted to one she barely knew.

"Probably because we met a week ago and have seen nothing of each other since," she replied with that daring smile. Her boldness was unusual. She had never been forward with men. Oh, sure, she'd kidded around with Hale a lot, but none of her flirtatious remarks to Hale—or any other male friend—had even come close to containing the messages she was knowingly sending Shep.

Before he could respond to that partially accusatory comment, she held up her empty glass. "Do you think I could I have a refill?"

Relieved that he didn't immediately have to come up with some sort of explanation as to why they hadn't seen each other since Christmas, Shep rose to his feet. "I'll get the bottle."

Andrea sighed happily as he went to the kitchen. Not in a hundred years could she have imagined this New Year's Eve. She had thought of Shep off and on since Christmas Day, recalling, during sleepless moments in dark nights, his truly arousing good looks and wondering if he had perhaps already left town. Of course, she could have knocked on Lucas's door and found out, but something had always stopped her from being *that* forward. After all, other than that electrified handshake and a few devastating smiles on Christmas Day, Shep had done nothing to make her think he was interested.

Her expression became slightly smug and very thrilled; apparently she'd been wrong in that assumption. He wouldn't be here tonight if he wasn't interested, would he?

Shep returned with the bottle of champagne. Standing over her, he poured some in her glass, which she had held up to make it easy for him. He felt her eyes probing his and he tried not to reciprocate, but involuntarily his gaze eventually melded with hers.

Then, to his surprise, he heard himself saying, "You have very beautiful eyes."

Andrea thought she would melt on the spot. "I can say the same about you, Dr. Wilde." Her voice was husky with emotion, and her heart was beating with the craziest rhythm. It was happiness causing it, she thought, the most delirious happiness she had ever felt. Sensible or not, way too fast or not, she was falling in love.

Shep was shocked to also feel a melting sensation. No woman had ever looked at him the way Andrea was doing, as though he were the most special man ever created. With a hammering heartbeat, he broke their overwhelming eye contact and hurried over to his chair. Dry mouthed, he quickly refilled his glass and took a healthy swallow.

He should leave, he thought next. If he didn't, if he stayed, something was going to happen, and it was something that shouldn't happen. It was in the air, in his body, in Andrea's eyes.

But he didn't get up from his chair and he didn't leave. It was as though he suddenly had no self-control. He'd arrived with self-control; he was positive of it. When he'd knocked on Andrea's door, he had honestly only been thinking of being with someone, anyone, at midnight on this last night of the year. He hadn't expected her to rush away and turn herself into this exquisitely beautiful woman, and for certain he hadn't expected the kind of smiles and looks she kept giving him.

Was she this way with every reasonably attractive man? He didn't like putting her and promiscuity in the same sentence, but what else could he think? And if that really was the case, how could he let her know how he felt about one-night stands without insulting her?

Maybe some normal conversation would alleviate the sexual tension in the room.

"Tell me," he said casually, "how did you end up in Rocky Ford?"

Andrea's stomach sank while her pulse suddenly raced. She didn't want to lie to Shep about anything. Something important was developing between them, and keeping their budding relationship on the right track seemed crucial.

But however much she wished she could be honest with him, the truth got stuck in her throat. Until she faced Charlie herself, until that fateful event occurred and was behind her, she could not speak of it to anyone. Shep might tell Lucas, and Lucas might mention it to someone else.

The thought of Charlie hearing through the grapevine about a woman in town claiming to be his daughter was abhorrent.

Recalling the story she had told Kathleen Osterman the other day over virtually the same question, she decided it would do for Shep, as well.

She forced a smile, though it came off rather weakly. "My mother passed away last February. Her estate demanded a lot of attention and required some travel."

"Did she own property around here?"

"Uh...no. I came here because...well, it was brought about by a problem of a...personal nature."

Shep's curiosity showed on his face. "When was it you came to Montana?"

"Last June."

"Must be a heck of a problem to keep you here that long."

Andrea cleared her throat. "It's...almost resolved."

"When it is, do you plan to return to California?"

She had answered all the questions on this topic that she could bear. Turning the tables on him, she asked, "Are you?"

Shep looked startled. "Am I what?"

"Going to return to California?"

He tossed back the champagne in his glass in one swallow. Then, with a dour expression, he said, "I don't know." His eyes suddenly narrowed on her. "Dad told you about my divorce, didn't he?" The look on Andrea's face was answer enough. Getting up to refill his glass, Shep growled, "I wish he hadn't done that."

Andrea rushed to Lucas's defense. "I'm sure he mentioned it only because he was worried about you, Shep. Believe me, he said nothing derogatory about you or your ex-wife, nor did he give me any private or personal details."

Absentmindedly Shep also refilled Andrea's glass. He sat down again and stared into the fire. "I didn't know you two were such close friends that he would talk about me and my problems. I mean, I knew you were friends, but..." His voice trailed off on an unhappy note.

"Please don't be upset by it," Andrea said softly. "Your father is a wonderful man. He has certainly been kind to me. I'm sure he never meant to step on your toes by conveying his concern. Your unexpected appearance on Christmas took him by surprise, Shep. And since he had proudly boasted about your professional success, and your marital happiness, many times over the months, he possibly felt some sort of explanation regarding your solitary arrival was necessary.

"It wasn't," she added quietly after a pause. "But maybe he thought it was."

Shep sucked in a long breath. Then he turned his head and looked at her with a dark and angry expression. "Are you dying to hear the gory details?"

It was almost as though he were attacking her, and his attitude stunned her. They should not be talking about either his past or hers. Not tonight. Tonight they should be gay and lighthearted. She could feel the effects of the champagne—her head was spinning from it—and the conversation had gotten entirely too serious. The whole evening could be ruined, and she didn't want that.

"Shep, I do not pry into other people's lives. No, I am not dying to hear details, gory or otherwise. Let's change the subject."

He glowered at her for a moment, then visibly relaxed. "Fine. You choose it."

She looked at her Christmas tree and got up. "I should have turned on the lights before this." Locating the switch, she pushed it, and the tiny lights began twinkling on and off. "I almost took it down this morning." She gave an indulgent little laugh. "Every morning since Christmas, to be factual. There was really no reason to leave it up, and I was concerned about it drying out. But it's sitting in a small pot, which I've kept adding water to, so the tree still looks healthy, don't you think?"

Shep wasn't looking at the tree. Neither was he thinking of the tree. The silent television screen displayed merrymakers in some city, and the music coming from the CD player was slow and sensuous. He would have to be numb from the neck down to be unaware of Andrea's magnetism, and parts of him might be numb—his heart, for instance—but the rest of his body was working just fine.

He took a swallow from his glass, then set it on the floor next to his chair. Rising, he took the few steps to the tree and Andrea.

Realizing he was right behind her, she turned and looked at him with big eyes.

"Care to dance?" he asked.

Just like that, she was happy again. Excited. "Yes, I would love to dance."

They assumed the traditional position and began moving slowly to the music. Andrea thought her heart might explode in her chest. She wasn't exactly in Shep Wilde's arms, but she was close. Looking up into his bottomless, dark eyes was a thrill beyond measure. Oh, yes, wise or not, she was falling very hard, very fast, for this man.

She felt pretty and carefree and alive, and she hadn't felt any of those sensations in a very long time. There was very little space for dancing, what with the Christmas tree crowding the small room, but Shep was barely moving his feet and she was following his lead.

And he kept looking into her eyes, perhaps the biggest thrill of all. She tried to breathe normally, but it was impossible. Every cell in her body seemed to be yearning for something, and while she didn't think of precise words or terms, she knew what that something was.

"This . . . this is nice," she said in a husky voice.

He pulled her closer. "But this is nicer."

Her face was against his chest. She could hear the hard, fast beating of his heart. "Much nicer," she whispered. She extracted her hand from his and slid both of hers up his chest to wind around his neck.

Shep drew a deep breath. She was pressed against him, and she felt and smelled heavenly. This was what she wanted, and it was beginning to be what he wanted, too. Why worry about tomorrow? he thought. Why should he worry about anything? Andrea was a big, all-grown-up girl. She knew what she was doing, same as he did. It was New Year's Eve, and maybe they both needed someone tonight.

No *maybe* about it, he thought next. He hadn't come over here with sex on the brain—not consciously, at any rate—but it was deeply embedded in his system now. If Andrea had merely said yes to bringing in the New Year together and done nothing to excite his libido, they wouldn't be dancing and he wouldn't be so aroused that she had to know it.

So it was really all her doing. He was only human, after all.

Andrea felt his mouth and breath in her hair, and she dreamily closed her eyes. His feelings for her went as deep as hers for him, she thought ecstatically. Sometimes fate was too cruel to bear, and then there were times like this. Lucas had talked about his son so often, and she had always listened, of course, but never could she have imagined Dr. Shepler Wilde as being so handsome and sexy. And what else was it but fate that had prompted her dinner invitation to Lucas for Christmas Day, and then Shep showing up on that very day and coming to her house with his father?

She snuggled closer to Shep's warm body. His arousal was evident and exciting. His arms tightened around her, and she could hear his irregular breathing. She was on cloud nine, floating in a sensual haze, somewhat reinforced by the champagne she had drunk.

But even without champagne, she knew she would be feeling the same delicious, overwhelming desire in Shep's arms. It was him she was drunk on, not the champagne.

The song they had been dancing to ended, and another began. But it had a faster beat, and Shep didn't start dancing again.

Instead, he laid his hands on each side of her head and looked into her eyes. "You know what's happening here, don't you?"

"Yes," she whispered. Her glowing smile reached her eyes. She knew he was going to kiss her, and she rose up on tiptoes to bring their lips closer together.

That was all Shep could take. His mouth covered hers in a kiss of utter possession. Andrea's heart pounded wildly as she kissed him back in the same hungry way. There was barely time for a breath of air between that first kiss and the second. His hands left her head to roam her back and hips.

"Shep...oh, Shep," she managed to whisper raggedly between the second and third kisses.

Then she lost count. She was barely aware of being backed up against a wall, and only dimly cognizant of him sliding her skirt up and then lifting one of her legs to wind it around his.

But his hand pushing her panties aside brought everything into sharp focus, maybe because he wasn't kissing her, but rather watching her face as he stroked her most sensitive spot. She stared back, and the passion she saw in his eyes increased her own to the boiling point.

"Tell me you want this," he demanded gruffly, hoarsely.

Her lips were parted to take in gasping breaths. "How can you doubt it?"

"Tell me. Say it."

"I want it. I want *you.*" She proved it by unbuttoning and unzipping his jeans and taking his hard manhood in her hand.

That was it for Shep. She could have said to stop, she could have said no; he'd given her the opportunity to say something that would have ended this. Instead, she had done the opposite. So be it.

For a few moments, he accepted the pleasurable movement of her hand on him, but then he wanted more. Kissing her mouth again, he adjusted their positions so that he was between her legs and sliding into her. He groaned out loud at the tightness of her body squeezing around his, at the heat and moisture he had encountered.

"You're perfect. Perfect," he muttered gutturally.

She took his compliment to heart and only thought that he, too, was perfect. Perfect in every way.

Her dress was going to be terribly wrinkled, possibly ruined. She didn't care. Never had she made love against a wall before. It was wonderful. He made love to her roughly, moving her this way and that to suit his fancy. She loved it.

Perspiring and moaning, she writhed with him. Sometimes one of her shoes touched the floor, and sometimes both feet were wrapped around him. She tore at the buttons of his shirt, and when it was open and his chest was bare, she nipped at it with her teeth and lips.

Everything in the room spun dizzily—the Christmas tree with its twinkling lights, the furniture, the fire in the fireplace. The music from the CD was in the background somewhere, not nearly loud enough to overcome the power of her wildly erotic thoughts: she loved this man. She had never been in love before, not like this. If he loved her only half as much as she did him, they would live happily ever after.

She wound her hands in his hair as he nuzzled her breasts. His breathing—and her own—would wake the dead. He was an expert contortionist, and though she'd never known it, so was she. Whatever else they did, Shep never stopped moving his hips, nor did she ever stop meeting his thrusts with her own.

She could feel the mounting tension in the pit of her stomach. It was going to happen soon, and she reached for it, concentrated on it. After so much promise, without that final, glorious release, she would surely wither and die.

"Shep . . . Shep," she whimpered. "Don't stop. Never stop."

"Don't worry about that, baby," he growled. He began moving faster, harder.

She felt the spasms begin, that spiraling pleasure that became stronger with each thrust of his body. "It's happening," she cried. "Yes . . . oh, yes."

It was happening for him, too. "Baby . . . *baby!*" It was a cry of supreme pleasure, and as suddenly as one turned off a light bulb, it was over. He all but collapsed on the floor. Making love in this crazy manner was a most definite test of strength, and he'd pretty much used his up in holding Andrea's weight—slight as it was—and satisfying them both.

They did end up on the floor, but only because they slid down to it together. Andrea, too, was weak. Shaky, as well. Trembling from the force of her climax and the physical effort exerted during their wild ride.

But she had never been happier in her life. Tenderly she laid a hand on Shep's cheek and smiled. "We are both a mess," she said teasingly.

It was true. His jeans were tangled around his knees, his shirt hanging from his shoulders. Her beautiful dress was no longer fit for mixed company. Her hair had come unpinned and was in her eyes, and she couldn't possibly have even a speck of makeup left on her face.

To her surprise, Shep didn't smile back over their disarray or her teasing comment. "Are you all right?" she asked quietly, feeling the first stages of a developing premonition . One that she suspected she wasn't going to like.

He pushed away from her, got to his feet and hiked up his jeans. "May I use your bathroom?"

Mutely she nodded, then said, "Down the hall."

Frowning, she watched him leave the room, remembering that he knew where the bathroom was because of Christmas. What was really on her mind, however, was that she needed the bathroom much more than he did, as they hadn't used protection.

"Damn," she whispered. They had just taken a terrible risk. Aside from the possibility of pregnancy, neither of them knew the other very well. A *stupid* risk in this day and age.

And he was a doctor. He knew better.

Well, she wasn't a doctor, but she knew better, too.

"Damn," she said again.

Shep walked in. Andrea scrambled to her feet and made a mad dash from the room. He picked up his glass, drained it and went to the champagne bottle for more. Holding up the bottle to the light, he eyeballed its contents: there was enough left for a few more drinks. "Good," he mumbled, and filled his glass.

In the bathroom, Andrea had the shakes. Something was wrong. Shep had not acted like a lover once the hottest sex she had ever experienced was over. Hadn't it been as good for him? She was not an expert on the subject and couldn't help wondering if it was possible for a woman to get so much from a sexual union and the man get very little.

And yet, if she had to venture an opinion on Shep's enjoyment quotient during their lovemaking, she would have to rate it as very high.

It was puzzling and upsetting and confusing, and she wanted to get back to Shep as quickly as she could. Maybe a few words from him would relieve her anxiety. Hurriedly repairing the damage to her appearance, she tried to think, with clarity, of every possible reason for his coolness after the fact.

The truth was that she couldn't read Shep Wilde. He was an enigma, cold as a winter morn one minute and hot as Hades the next.

Finally, reasonably put back together, she returned to the living room. She had exchanged her wrinkled dress for a robe, but otherwise looked pretty much the same as she had before their bout of intense lovemaking. She desperately wanted to hear something nice from Shep, something that would stop the trembling in her system.

He was standing with his back to the fire and his glass in his hand. Their eyes met. She tried to smile; he didn't.

She was suddenly embarrassed and, merely for something to do, she picked up her own glass and took a sip.

"Are you staring at me for a reason?" she asked, speaking calmly though there was nothing calm about her emotions. In fact, she felt on the verge of tears and didn't know why.

"You're very beautiful," he said tonelessly.

"And that's why you're staring?"

"Maybe. Maybe I'm wishing you weren't."

"That makes no sense at all."

"You're right, it doesn't. But not much does these days. What we just did sure as hell doesn't."

Her premonition became stronger and more painful. "What's that supposed to mean?"

"We're practically strangers. I didn't come over here for sex. What do you think it means?"

"I haven't the foggiest. Suppose you tell me." Her head was beginning to ache, and she set her glass down, wishing with all her heart that she hadn't drunk so much champagne.

Shep took a long breath. "Yes, I *have* to tell you. It's this. I'm sorrier than I can say for what happened between us. It was entirely my fault, and—"

"Your fault!" She took a step toward him. "It was no more your fault than mine. And just why are you sorry? That's what's important, Shep, and what I'd like to hear. Why are you sorry?"

He looked at her for a long time, then his eyes dropped. "Because it can't go anywhere."

She felt as though she'd just received a blow. "You mean, that was it. Wham, bam, thank you ma'am, or something to that effect?"

"Please don't be bitter. You're Dad's friend, and I wouldn't intentionally hurt you for the world."

She folded her arms across her chest, deliberately assuming a militant stance. "Why on earth would you think I'm hurt? I got what I wanted, didn't I? Incidentally, you performed beautifully." Her smile dripped sarcasm. "You've got what it takes to satisfy a woman, Dr. Wilde. I'd bet anything you've never had a complaint, am I right?"

Shep set his glass on the mantel. "I think I'd better be going."

"What? You're not going to see in the New Year with me? And there I thought we might try doing it on the kitchen table right after we drank a toast at midnight."

"Andrea, please."

"Please, my left foot! You conceited, amoral jerk. Do you think I sleep with just anybody? I've never had a one-night stand in my life, or I didn't until tonight."

"I'm sorry. What more can I say?" Shep was at the closet, getting his jacket. This was much worse than he'd anticipated. Obviously, he'd been wrong in thinking that Andrea took her pleasure wherever she found it. But she'd come on so strong. Why wouldn't he question her standards and respond to her blatant invitations? The curving fullness of her lips would make any man think of kissing them, and, of course, kisses led to other intimacies.

And she'd never said no, nor so much as hesitated. Not once. He sighed, then dared to look at her again. The daggers in her eyes seemed real enough to stab a man right through his heart. But there was something besides murder in those beautiful eyes—little-girl hurting.

Dammit, he thought violently, despising himself at that moment.

"Good night," he mumbled, hurrying from the room and through the kitchen to the back door.

The last thing he heard in Andrea Dillon's house was a piercing, cynical, bitter "Happy New Year, sport!" from her.

He hiked through the snow to his dad's house, feeling like a dog.

Five

____

Shep saw the New Year in while lying in bed, wide-awake, in the dark, in the same bedroom he'd slept in throughout childhood, high school and until he went away to college. Since Natalie's desertion, he'd believed that he could not have been more miserable. Tonight he'd found out there was always one more degree of misery. All a person had to do to attain it was to behave like an ass.

In truth, his behavior since the moment Natalie had asked for a divorce was nothing to be proud of. Letting his lucrative medical practice slip away. Giving in to Natalie's ridiculous financial demands. Coming to his dad's home to lick his wounds like a damned kid. No, he wasn't proud of any of it.

Tonight was the topper. He had plied a decent young woman with champagne and taken advantage of her affection for him. Then he'd insulted her with an apology. What in hell was wrong with him? He used to be a pretty nice guy.

"Before Natalie," he muttered. And before he'd changed his professional goals because of her whims, and before he'd started making more money than he'd ever dreamed of earning, and before the fancy house and medical offices, the showy cars, the phony friends. He'd let it all happen. Him, Shep Wilde, no one else. He could have stood up to Natalie when she'd pouted because he had wanted to limit his practice. He could have refused her father's financial assistance in getting started.

He could have been a man.

But it was all water under the bridge, wasn't it?

For the first time, he realized that was exactly what his past was—water under the bridge and gone forever. It was time to shape up, to take hold of his life and do something with it. He had paid his dues. Maybe he was a better man for it, maybe not. But he was educated, and a doctor could always find a job. It might not be exactly what one hoped for, but then, did he have any particular hopes about his career anymore?

The important thing was to get back to work in some field of medicine. From there, who knew what might happen?

It was three in the morning before he finally got sleepy.

At least one good thing had come from the night's fiasco: a decision to look for a job.

It beat driving for hours without a destination, or hanging around his dad's house like a mindless moron, by a mile.

For Andrea, New Year's Day seemed to drag. She'd never been more depressed in her life, knew it, worried about it and fought the feeling as hard as she could.

But it was persistent and survived a long walk in the snow, attempts at reading, watching television and listening to music, cooking a meal she could barely choke down and even some housecleaning. At one point, around four in the afternoon, she actually sat down with her atlas and thumbed through the pages and states, looking for someplace to move to. She never wanted to see Shep Wilde's face again, and if they both stayed in Rocky Ford, they were bound to run into each other. She doubted very much that

Shep would tell Lucas about last night, and Lucas himself might set up some event that would bring them all together.

In the end, though, she closed the atlas with a frustrated sigh. She couldn't leave Rocky Ford yet. Not with her cowardice regarding meeting Charlie Fanon hanging over her head like a heavy, dark cloud, she couldn't.

Pacing, frowning and taut with tension, she concluded that if she once worked up her courage and went to see Charlie, then she could leave town with at least a modicum of self-satisfaction, whatever his reaction.

Besides, it galled her to think that a sudden move now would mean that she had let Shep drive her away. She had as much right to live where she did as Lucas did. Shep was the intruder, damn his black soul. Why hadn't he stayed in California where he belonged? So what if he wasn't happy over his divorce? Why run home to Daddy? People got divorced every day, and few of them perished from the experience.

Andrea had to amend a portion of those angry thoughts and questions. Shep had come home, true, but in all honesty she couldn't believe that he'd "run home to Daddy." He wasn't the type and, in fact, seemed to be just the opposite, a cold-hearted bastard who needed no one, not even his own father. Small wonder he was divorced. Given his completely self-focused personality, it was a wonder that he'd found a woman who would marry him in the first place.

But, oh Lord, he made incredible love.

Groaning because she was a damned fool to even form such a thought, Andrea got up and brought the atlas to the bookcase.

It was already getting dark outside, another snowy, wintry night. Even though she doubted she would sleep any better tonight than she had last night, she took a hot bath, gulped down an over-the-counter sleeping pill and went to bed.

She would deal with tomorrow—and the next tomorrow and the next—when it came.

What else could she do?

* * *

Around ten the following morning, Andrea's phone rang. Her heart skipped a beat; it had to be Lucas, Shep or a wrong number. Or one of those salespeople whose computers dialed sequential numbers, she added to herself while gingerly approaching the instrument.

It was vexing to realize that some traitorous part of herself was hoping to hear Shep's voice on the line. But her sensible side voided that hope, and it was with great reluctance that she picked up the receiver. "Hello?"

"Hello, Andrea. Kathleen Osterman here. Do you have a few minutes to chat?"

Perplexed, Andrea sank into a nearby chair. "Did I leave my phone number at your office, Ms. Osterman?"

"No, but I have a friend at the phone company."

"And he gave you my unlisted number?"

"Please don't let it upset you. He would never give it to anyone else, I assure you. Andrea, you mentioned some articles you had written that were published in your college paper. I'd like to see them."

"You would?" Andrea winced at her immature response. But this call was so surprising, and Kathleen's request to see her articles even more so. "Certainly you may see them," she said in a more controlled voice. "Shall I bring them to your office?"

"Actually, I'd like you to bring them to my home. Would you mind?"

"Not at all. Just tell me where and when."

"My home is seven miles west of town on Grandview Road. It's a large brick house with several outbuildings. My name is on the mailbox. I'm sure you won't have any trouble locating it. And if you don't have other plans, Andrea, I'd like you to come for lunch. Twelve o'clock should do it."

Andrea's initial surprise felt like an inflating balloon, just getting bigger and bigger. "I have no other plans, Ms. Osterman. I'll be there."

"Wonderful, and please call me Kathleen."

"As you wish. See you at noon."

Andrea put down the phone and mumbled, "Well, for heaven's sake. What brought that on?"

Whatever it was, it was exciting. Andrea's downcast spirits had risen considerably. Lunch at Kathleen's home so she could read her published articles had to mean something. What was Kathleen thinking? Was there a job at the *Rocky Ford News* in Andrea's future?

"Oh, my," she whispered, thrilled over the possibility. Getting up, she ran to her bedroom closet to pick out something to wear. Then she made a quick U-turn and ran to find her articles.

Nervous as a cat, it took her over an hour to get ready.

She finally backed out of her driveway and headed for Grandview Road muttering thanks to the powers-that-be that it wasn't snowing today, or worse, blowing *and* snowing. In fact, for a cold winter day, it was rather pleasant. The sun was bright, making the snowbanks on each side of the road sparkle like tiny diamonds.

And she knew in her heart that something good was going to come out of this meeting—she just knew it.

Well, she was certainly ready for something good, she thought wryly. Almost the entire year had been the pits, starting with her mother's death. She'd been at work when the fateful telephone call came. *Miss Dillon, we found your name with several phone numbers in Sandra Worthington's billfold. Are you a relative?*

Sandra had been in her car, driving on a busy street, when she had suffered a brain hemorrhage. She had died almost instantly, the doctors told Andrea later.

The series of shocks Andrea had undergone for weeks after had started with that phone call. She tossed her head, flipping her hair back from her face, putting the whole awful ordeal out of her mind.

But her ordeal wasn't over yet, was it? she thought next. Not until she stood face-to-face with Charlie Fanon and told him who she was would it be over. When she left Kathleen's home today, she should take the shortest possible route to Charlie's house, walk in and boldly introduce herself.

Her stomach quivered, and her hands were suddenly clammy.

She would think about it later.

Shep walked into his father's house wearing a smile. Lucas smiled back, happy to see his son smiling instead of scowling. Something was up. Shep was dressed in a suit and topcoat instead of his usual jeans.

Removing his coat, Shep said, "I have some good news, Dad."

Lucas's grin broadened. "I knew it the minute I saw you. What is it?"

"I've got a job at the hospital."

"*Our* hospital?" Clearly, Lucas was surprised.

"In the emergency room, Dad."

"But that's not your specialty."

"It was the only opening."

"You told them you're a plastic surgeon, didn't you?"

"I showed the administrator all of my credentials. But it's a small hospital, and they can't afford to put a plastic surgeon on the staff. The emergency room is fine, Dad. I'm glad to get the job. I'll be working some peculiar hours, but that's fine, too. At least I'll be working."

Lucas sat back in his chair. "You're planning to stay in Rocky Ford. I'm glad, son."

"Well, I'm planning to stay for the time being. I can't promise anything, Dad."

"I understand. Will you continue living with me? Sure hope so."

"That's something I didn't think about. Are you sure you want me underfoot?"

"Shep, having you underfoot is a blessing. Please don't rush out and find an apartment or something."

Shep laid his hand on his father's shoulder. "Okay, Dad. I won't move out if you promise me one thing. If I get on your nerves and you decide you'd rather be living alone again, you'll tell me."

"It'll never happen, Shep."

"Promise me, Dad."

"All right, I promise. When do you start at the hospital?"

"Tonight. Eleven o'clock."

"Hell of a time to start a shift."

Shep nodded, but he was thinking that 11:00 p.m. was a darned good time for a guy with insomnia to start a shift.

A strange woman opened Kathleen's front door after Andrea rang the bell.

"You're Andrea Dillon?" the woman asked.

"Yes."

"Come in. Kathleen's expecting you."

Andrea stepped into a large, elegant foyer, and the woman shut the door. "I'm Ruth Madison, Kathleen's housekeeper. Let me take your coat."

Shedding the garment, Andrea handed it over. "Thank you."

"You're quite welcome. Kathleen's in the library. Through that door, Miss Dillon."

"Thank you."

Andrea raised her hand to rap on the door and heard Ruth say, "Just go in, Miss Dillon. You don't have to knock. Kathleen heard your car. She knows you're here."

Nodding, Andrea turned the knob and walked in. To her surprise, Kathleen was lying on the sofa with a blanket over her legs.

"Hello, Andrea," Kathleen said. "Come in and find a seat. That green chair would be best. I wouldn't have to turn my head to see you."

"Are you ill?" Andrea was confused. If Kathleen was ill today, why had she invited a guest for lunch?

Kathleen's smile was desert dry. "I suppose I am, although I don't feel ill. Please sit down, Andrea."

Andrea took the green chair and looked around. "This is a lovely room."

"I'm glad you like it. It's my favorite. Do you have your articles?"

"Right here." Andrea had brought a shoulder bag large enough to hold a letter-sized manila envelope. She took the envelope from her purse, got up and carried it over to Kathleen.

At the same moment, Ruth came in with a large tray. "We're going to have lunch in here, Andrea. Ruth will set you up at that small table, and I'll eat from a tray."

This was most peculiar to Andrea. Only last week, Kathleen had struck her as a dynamo. Today the paleness around her mouth and the shadowy circles under her eyes came through her makeup. She had on a bulky sweater the same vivid blue as her eyes, and her hair was as stylish as Andrea remembered.

But there were too many clues for Andrea not to suspect a serious illness. She couldn't blurt out her curiosity and concern, of course. If and when Kathleen wanted her to know what was wrong, she would tell her.

Efficiently Ruth laid out Andrea's lunch. Kathleen's small tray contained a bowl of clear broth and some soda crackers, while Andrea's plate was laden with a sandwich, a mound of macaroni salad, pickles, celery and black olives.

Kathleen pulled the newspaper clippings from the envelope. "I'll read these while you eat, Andrea."

Ruth spoke. "I have a nice pot of herbal tea steeping for Kathleen, Miss Dillon, but if you prefer something else to drink..."

"Tea is fine, Ruth, thank you."

Ruth bustled away to get the tea. Uneasily Andrea sat at the small round table to eat her lunch. She was no longer in Kathleen's line of vision, which gave Andrea the opportunity to watch the newswoman reading her college articles. She was beginning to get the strangest feeling: Kathleen's sudden interest in her writing ability had something to do with her illness.

Andrea picked up her fork and took a bite of the macaroni salad, and noticed Kathleen absentmindedly nibbling a soda cracker. She seemed to be intent on her reading, and Andrea couldn't help wondering if she perceived any journalistic talent in the articles.

Ruth brought in another tray, bearing a teapot, cups, cream, sugar and lemon. After serving the tea, she left again.

Andrea tried to eat, and the food was very good, but her stomach was churning a bit sickishly and her mind was so confused over this rather bizarre luncheon date that she mostly sat there, sipped tea and worried.

Finally Kathleen lowered the last clipping. For several moments—they seemed an eternity to Andrea—Kathleen said nothing, just stared into space and appeared to be thinking very hard.

Then she turned her head and looked at Andrea. "You're a good writer. Concise, articulate without being too wordy and rather lively. Some of the topics in these articles are dull as dishwater, but you made them interesting."

"They were assigned to me, Kathleen. Only occasionally was a student reporter permitted to choose a subject to write about." Andrea got up and returned to the green chair for Kathleen's benefit. Her praise felt like a shower of flowers and had indeed elevated Andrea's hopes.

"Sounds standard for college papers," Kathleen remarked.

"At any rate, I appreciate your very kind words about my work," Andrea murmured. "Thank you."

"They're also true words, Andrea. I wasn't merely flattering you to hear the sound of my own voice. And if I hadn't liked your work, I would have said so in no uncertain terms."

Andrea had to smile. "I believe you."

"Please do. Now, here's the situation. My doctors tell me that I must have an operation. In fact, if I'd given them their way, I would be in the hospital right now. What I had to make them understand—no small feat, incidentally—was that I could not permit my newspaper to fall apart just because I would be laid up for a month or so.

"My husband and I started the *Rocky Ford News* thirty-two years ago, Andrea. The town had around eight hundred residents, so you might well imagine what our income was. Fortunately, money wasn't a problem. Greg, my husband, had inherited a great deal of money, and the only thing he really wanted to do with it was to own and operate a newspaper. We were very young and very much in love.''

Kathleen smiled nostalgically. ''For some reason, Greg also loved the Rocky Ford area. He'd been born and raised in Billings, but there was something about this place he couldn't get over. Anyhow, I dove into the project because of him, but it wasn't long before I had the same feverish affection for the business that he did. My, those were wonderful years.''

She drew herself up. ''That's neither here nor there. I have good help at the paper, Andrea, but not one on-site writer. Keeping that particular delight all to myself has come home to haunt me. Oh, I know my employees could fill the paper with wire-service articles, and, of course, there are the free-lancers scattered around the area.

''But some things, some events, require a real writer—the town's political arena, for example. Right now, there's a hassle going on in the town council over flood control and building a decent bridge across Access Creek. That creek is both a blessing and a curse. The water is crucial to the survival of several ranches, but it's a menace when it overflows its banks. As for the bridge, what's there now is safe only for cars, and yet ranchers have to drive trucks across it to carry supplies to their homes. And to move animals to market. It's a dangerous situation and a point of particular contention with me.''

''I've been following your articles about the creek, Kathleen.'' Andrea smiled. ''For that matter, I read every issue of your paper from first page to last.'' Her heart was beating with an internal excitement. Kathleen was going to offer her a job. Andrea could never be glad that someone's illness was of benefit to her, but the thought of working again, and this time actually writing about current and newsworthy events, and of seeing her work in the newspaper—with her byline, she hoped—was exhilarating.

''One would think finding a reporter would be an easy task,'' Kathleen said. ''I know so many, being in the business for so long. But if they're any good, they're already working, and while I love Rocky Ford and my newspaper, I have to concede that moving here and working for me would be a step down for most of my friends."

Her piercing blue eyes bored into Andrea. "You wouldn't consider it a step down, would you?"

Andrea laughed. "From no job at all to reporting the local news? No, Kathleen, I would not consider it a step down." The elation in her system was almost more than she could conceal.

"Well, do you think you can handle it?"

"Are you offering me a job, Kathleen?"

"Your experience is so limited, I don't mind admitting that I'm not thrilled about it, but yes, I'm offering you a job. You would not be interfering with the other employees' work, and I have already turned over the accounting and business end of the paper to Dave Collins. He's the accountant who's been doing my taxes for many years, but I've always kept the daily records myself. Anyhow, your duties would consist solely of gathering and writing the important local news. Since you've been reading my paper so diligently, you know what I consider important."

"I happily accept your offer," Andrea stated with a calmness she certainly didn't feel.

"Without discussing salary?" Kathleen asked wryly.

"I'm sure you'll be fair."

"And money isn't an issue," Kathleen added. "Wasn't that what you said in my office that day?"

"I did say that, yes."

"So, you're like Greg was, independently wealthy and in love with the newspaper business."

"I'm not wealthy, Kathleen, but I have enough money to comfortably get by," Andrea said quietly.

"You don't like talking about it. Neither did Greg."

"What happened to Mr. Osterman, Kathleen."

"He died fourteen years ago. Heart attack. Same thing the doctors are attempting to prevent happening to me."

"You have heart problems?"

"A whole slew of them. I don't want to think about it. Your salary will be three hundred dollars a week. I'd like you to start tomorrow morning, eight sharp. You may use my office and desk. You'll find all sorts of notes to myself in that desk. Use them."

Kathleen's medical problems were much more serious than Andrea had thought. She suddenly wasn't quite so elated.

"Is your surgery scheduled?" she asked in a subdued tone of voice.

"Day after tomorrow. I'll be going into the hospital in Missoula tomorrow morning. Andrea, when I'm clear-headed again, I'll be calling the paper and will want to speak to everyone there, including you."

"I understand."

Kathleen looked at her for a long time, then said, "Please don't disappoint me. I'm putting a lot of faith and trust in someone I hardly know."

"I realize that and I appreciate it. I won't disappoint you, Kathleen. I promise."

"You may go now. I'm very tired."

Andrea got to her feet. Kathleen *looked* very tired. "I'm so sorry you're ill," Andrea said quietly.

There wasn't much humor in Kathleen's off-center grin. "Not as sorry as I am, young woman." After a beat, she added quite calmly, "There is a chance I won't survive the surgery. You should probably know that. If that happens, Dave Collins will step in and put the newspaper up for sale, as I have no heirs. The proceeds will go to the University of Montana. Don't look so shocked, Andrea. We all have to go sometime. And I've given explicit instructions to Dave that the paper is not to close. You're guaranteed a job until the new owners take over, if that be the case. He, they or whatever would then decide your and my other employees' fate."

Andrea's eyes and nose were stinging from unshed tears. Her voice was unsteady. "I'm sure you'll be all right, Kathleen. You're a fighter."

Kathleen gave a brittle little laugh. "You're right about that. Run along now. I'm in desperate need of a nap."

With her purse over her shoulder, Andrea said, "Good-bye for now, and thank you. I'll be expecting your first call in a few days."

Kathleen's eyes were already closed, and she didn't answer. Andrea slipped out of the room, closed the door, then weakly leaned against the foyer wall.

Ruth appeared. "Is she all right?"

"She's sleeping." A sob welled in her throat and escaped. "I had no idea when I came here today...."

"I know."

Andrea pushed herself away from the wall. "I'll be going now. I'm sure we'll see each other again, Ruth. Thank you for lunch."

"You're welcome."

Andrea walked out of Kathleen's beautiful home and sucked in a massive breath of the cold air.

She drove home with a cacophony of feelings. She had a job, one she knew she was going to love, but what a terrible way of attaining it.

"Be well, Kathleen," she whispered. "Please be well."

Six

Shep was heading home after his eight-hour shift at the hospital. He was nearly there when he recognized an oncoming car as Andrea's. Tooting his horn, he waved as they passed by each other.

She didn't toot, didn't wave, didn't even look his way.

He frowned with a stirring of anger. Was this to be their relationship from now on? Did she intend to ignore him ad infinitum as punishment for his indiscretions on New Year's Eve?

He'd done nothing she hadn't wanted, he thought defensively. And he had tried to make amends for crossing the line with a heartfelt apology; what more did she want him to do?

"Probably eat dirt and die," he muttered. The whole affair was a thorn in his side. First of all, he didn't want Andrea angry with him. Then there was his own annoying memory, which kept dredging up that night and clicking off every tiny detail of their passionate lovemaking. A man didn't easily forget the kind of wildly erotic sex he and Andrea had shared.

And there was something else gnawing at him: he liked her. Yes, he'd realized that fact a little late, but ever since New Year's Eve, the knowledge had been growing on him.

He liked her, wanted at least her friendship, and she wouldn't even wave at him. How did a man change a woman's attitude toward him? He sure hadn't had any luck with Natalie in that regard; what made him think he would succeed with Andrea?

With a perplexed shake of his head, he turned into his dad's driveway. Lucas was in the kitchen when Shep walked in.

"Morning, son. How'd the job go?" were Lucas's first words.

Shep could smell the sausages simmering on the stove, and he was suddenly ravenously hungry. "It's as different as day is to night compared to a Los Angeles emergency room," he replied. "But it went fine, Dad. I'm going to wash up. Those sausages smell great."

They talked while they ate breakfast together. "Was it a long night?" Lucas asked.

"Seemed long. Around midnight, I treated some accident victims. A husband and wife, older folks. They're from Billings and were traveling south. Their pickup skidded into a snowbank about ten miles from town, and neither of them had been wearing a seat belt. They both hit the windshield and had some facial lacerations, but they were darned lucky they weren't seriously injured."

"So you sewed 'em up and let them go?"

"There was no reason to keep them in the hospital. Someone gave them a ride to a motel. They talked about getting their pickup dug out and towed to town in the morning. I think they were more worried about their truck than themselves." Shep shook his head. "Maybe they'll start using their seat belts. Hope they do."

"Anyone else come in?"

"A few people. Nothing serious. As I said, it sure isn't anything like an emergency room in L.A." He'd done his stint in emergency care during his training, and the emergency room in which he'd taken his training had been a madhouse. His biggest problem with this job was probably going to be boredom. He'd met the entire night staff at the hospital, wandered the wards and various departments to familiarize himself with the place and then read through several medical journals.

Oh, yes, he'd done one more thing last night: he'd thought about Andrea and New Year's Eve. Endlessly, so it seemed this morning.

And then she'd passed him on the street without so much as a nod.

"I saw Andrea's car heading for town on my way home," he said with studied nonchalance. "Where do you suppose she would be going so early?"

Lucas shrugged. He took a swallow of coffee and set his mug down again. "I've noticed that she sometimes comes and goes at odd hours. Middle of the night, even. Course, that's only if I happen to be awake and hear her car."

Shep's brow knit in perplexity. "Where on earth would she go in the middle of the night?"

"Beats me. She doesn't talk about herself much, Shep, and I never was one to pry into other folks' business. Her being out this morning seems pretty normal, though. It must have been around seven-thirty when you saw her."

"Yeah, it was," Shep concurred. He eyed his father. "You really don't know very much about her?"

Lucas slowly shook his head. "Nope, can't say that I do. I know her mother died last year. February, I think Andrea said. Then she came to Rocky Ford in the spring."

"And rented the house next door."

"No, it was sometime during the summer that she moved in."

"Where was she staying in the interim?"

Lucas shrugged again. "She never said. Maybe with friends."

Shep sat back in his chair. "I don't think she has any friends, Dad. Except for you."

"Aw, that can't be true, Shep. Nice girl like her? No, I can't believe that."

"Have you met any of her friends? Have you even seen anyone over there?"

"Well, I hardly hang on the fence to see what goes on next door, Shep."

"No, but you've heard her car leaving in the middle of the night. It's not impossible that you might have noticed a...a party, for instance. A bunch of cars parked around her place would be hard to miss. Ever see anything like that?"

"Shep, by any chance are you interested in my pretty next-door neighbor?" There was a teasing twinkle in Lucas's eyes.

Shep looked thoughtful for a moment. Then he shoved a forkful of pancake into his mouth and nodded. "Could be, Dad."

Lucas's grin was a yard wide. "You can't imagine how much that pleases me. Andrea's a wonderful young woman."

Shep smirked slightly. "How can you be so sure of that when you admittedly know so little about her?"

Lucas put on his most stubborn expression. "I just know it, Shep."

Shep relented. "Okay, Dad, I'll take your word for it." He got up from the table. "I'm going to bed. Thanks for the great breakfast."

Andrea parked her car and walked into the newspaper office with her heart in her throat. Would Kathleen's employees welcome her or consider her an intruder? Hopefully, Kathleen had told them to expect her.

Her anxieties were relieved when the two women in front greeted her warmly, and even the pressman left his domain to say hello. His name was Duane Kemp, and he was around forty years old, with a stern-looking face above a reed-thin body. A rather nice-looking man, really. Andrea shook hands with him.

Sally, the secretary, brought her a cup of coffee, and Grace, the woman who managed the classifieds, offered her a doughnut.

Andrea took the coffee and refused—with thanks—the doughnut. The women were full of questions—"Are you from around here?...Where did you live before coming to Montana?...Do you have family in the area?"—but Duane vanished immediately after the handshake.

Andrea fielded the questions well enough and finally managed to close herself into Kathleen's office.

It was an astounding place. Carrying her coffee, she inspected everything, the stacks of books and papers she had seen as clutter before, and the framed pictures and articles on the walls. One—a front page of the *Rocky Ford News*—was captioned Our First Publication. Hurrah! There were photos of Kathleen and people of prominence, politicians, film stars, television personalities and sports figures. Apparently, any person with a claim to fame who had even come close to the Rocky Ford area had been interviewed and photographed. Kathleen obviously let very little grass grow under her feet.

But Andrea's thoughts were complimentary, not derogatory. She admired Kathleen enormously. Perhaps more accurately, Andrea admired what Kathleen had accomplished in her lifetime. And her work had not gone unnoticed in the industry. The walls also contained plaques and written awards for outstanding achievement in the field of journalism.

And then Andrea came upon a most touching photograph. A very young and very beautiful Kathleen was smiling at a handsome, young, dark-haired man; he had to be Greg Osterman, Kathleen's deceased husband.

Andrea looked at the photo for a long time. The Ostermans' love for each other was right there in the picture with them, in plain sight for all to see. How marvelous.

Her thoughts went to Shep Wilde then, and she bit down painfully hard on her lower lip. He was the first man with whom she had immediately perceived a future. He was the first man she had made love with before knowing him inside and out. He was the *only* man she had fallen in love with at first sight.

After a moment, she tossed her head and went to sit at Kathleen's desk. Thinking of Shep was wasted time and usually gave her a headache. Certainly, it made her heart ache in a unique and all but unbearable manner. How had he had the gall to honk his car horn and wave at her this morning? Had he actually thought she would smile and wave back? Didn't he know how badly he had hurt her with his callous, arrogant apology?

She set down her cup and began opening drawers, looking for the notes Kathleen had mentioned. In all honesty, she didn't know where to begin in this job, and there was no one to help her out, either. The other employees had specific duties and were apparently very good at them. But they weren't writers or reporters, and she was going to have to find her own way.

Determination was suddenly her driving force. She *would* find her way and she *would* succeed in this job. Last but certainly not least, she would make Kathleen proud of her.

For some reason, Kathleen's approval seemed utterly crucial.

As tired as Shep was when he went to bed, he did not sleep soundly. Lying awake at intervals throughout the day, he faced what was eating at him and came to a decision: he would not rest easily until he and Andrea were on friendly terms. If she said no to anything beyond friendship between them, he would understand, but ignoring each other's existence was adolescent and ridiculous.

He got up around three, showered, shaved and dressed in clean clothing. Lucas had gone somewhere, and the house was vacant, he discovered upon leaving his bedroom and going to the kitchen. He made a pot of coffee and a sandwich, and read the local newspaper while he ate.

Then he put on his jacket and gloves and went outside. The sky was overcast, promising more snow, and it was cold. Having grown up in Rocky Ford, he remembered winters with almost daily storms and six- to ten-foot banks of snow. He also remembered winters with very little snow and mild temperatures. This, apparently, was one of the harsher years.

That was okay with him. He liked that nothing in the area reminded him of southern California. Maybe that was the real reason he'd come home to get himself back on some sort of track. Montana and the Los Angeles area were like two different planets. He might never have done any healing if he'd stayed in California. And to his way of thinking, taking a job and the responsibility that went with it was a positive step in the healing process.

So was liking another woman. Determinedly he set out for Andrea's house, going down Lucas's driveway, walking the short distance on the road to Andrea's driveway and then mounting the two steps to her front door. He hadn't used her front door before; rather, he'd plowed through the snow of their backyards and used the small opening in the fence that connected Lucas's and Andrea's properties. It was the way Lucas had taken him on Christmas Day and how he'd arrived on New Year's Eve.

Today he thought it best to present a more formal presence and knock on her front door.

Only, after knocking three times, he was frowning. Wasn't Andrea at home?

He couldn't tell from her car's absence in the driveway, as she kept it in the garage and the garage door was down.

Had she been gone all day? *Where* would she spend an entire day? With whom?

Surely she wasn't inside and just not answering the door because it was him on her stoop, was she?

He tried one more time, calling "Andrea?" while he knocked.

Everything remained silent. Turning away from the door, he surveyed her yard and garage. Spotting a small window in the garage, he hiked over to it and peered in. The garage was empty.

So she really had gone somewhere for the day, he thought uneasily. But where? To do what?

"Hell," he mumbled, and trudged back to his father's house.

Lucas came home a short time later. He'd been to the grocery store, and Shep helped him carry in the sacks of food.

"Did you have a good sleep?" Lucas asked, adding before Shep could answer, "Never did sleep very well during the day myself, except for a little nap now and then."

"I slept well enough," Shep said, which wasn't a total lie. Everything had been brought in from Lucas's car and was residing on the kitchen counters. Lucas took off his jacket and started putting things away. "I dropped in on Andrea," Shep said casually. "But she wasn't home."

Lucas sent him a glance over his shoulder. "Oh?"

Shep heaved a sigh. Obviously, Lucas found nothing peculiar about Andrea's extended absence. "I think she's been gone all day," he said, pressing his point, hoping Lucas would get it and say something like, *Oh, she visits a friend in Billings every so often,* or a comment to that effect.

"Could be" was all Lucas said, and quite calmly, to boot.

Feeling frustrated, Shep dropped the subject and began emptying a paper sack of its contents. Andrea would get home sooner or later.

He could only hope her arrival preceded his ten-thirty departure for the hospital.

Andrea's mind was so crammed with information about her job—for which she still hadn't found a starting line— her head and stomach both ached from nervous tension. She had spent hours reading Kathleen's notes, some of which were lengthy references to topics that Kathleen had obviously intended to pursue for articles for the paper, and others were merely a few words scratched on scraps of paper and made no sense at all to Andrea.

There had been an edition of the paper put out today; the next one would come out on Saturday. She had discussed what was already slated for the Saturday edition with Duane Kemp, and he had looked at her quizzically, Andrea recalled during the drive home. As if he'd been asking, *And what is your contribution going to be to Saturday's edition?*

Well, she had no contribution. Not even an idea for the editorial, which was always on page two of the paper, whereby Kathleen expressed her opinion on some controversial topic. In truth, Andrea didn't know what was controversial in Rocky Ford and what wasn't. She could always pick up on something from the wire services, of course, even an international incident, and let the newspaper's readers know how she felt about it. But she couldn't seem to get herself excited about that route to an editorial.

Actually, Kathleen's notes were more confusing than helpful. Andrea felt strung out and terribly disappointed with herself. Here she had been handed the opportunity to prove her worth as a newswoman, and she felt almost brain-dead. Where was her imagination? Surely she could take something from those notes and expand it into an interesting article or editorial.

At any rate, she had brought the manila envelope home with her. It resided on the seat next to her, along with her purse, and she kept casting it quick, wary glances. Since she had no ideas of her own for an article, she would *have* to use one of Kathleen's. Thank goodness she owned a laptop computer and had brought it to Montana with her. She would work all night, if necessary, and produce something good for Saturday's edition or die trying.

Pulling into her driveway, she pressed the button on the remote control to raise the garage door. It had started snowing around four, and it was coming down hard and piling up fast. Without question, she would have to shovel her driveway before leaving for work in the morning.

Sighing over so many trials and tribulations, Andrea drove into the garage, gathered her purse and the envelope and got out of her car. After pressing the wall button to close the door, she went into the house.

The first thing she did was plop down into her favorite chair in the living room. It felt so good to be home, she almost cried. The day had been draining. Hers was not an ordinary job. What had made Kathleen think she could handle it?

She was still sitting there in her coat, with her purse and the envelope on her lap, when someone knocked on the front door.

"Oh, no," she groaned, too exhausted to even feel her usual wariness when her phone rang or someone came to her door.

Pushing herself up and out of the chair, she left her purse and the envelope behind and went to the door in her coat. "Who's there?" she called.

"It's Shep. I need to talk to you."

He might need to talk to her, but talking to him was the last thing *she* needed. "Sorry," she said flatly. "Not interested."

"Andrea, please. Open the door. I only want a few minutes of your time."

She heaved a weary sigh. "Shep, go away. I worked all day, I'm tired and—"

"You worked? Doing what?"

"That's none of your business." Shouting through the heavy door was silly, but why didn't he just go away and leave her be? Hadn't he inflicted enough damage on her ego? What more did he want from her?

"Andrea, do you have a job? If you do, it's really strange because I have a job, too. Isn't that a peculiar coincidence?"

Andrea frowned, but her curiosity had definitely been piqued. She unlocked the door and pulled it open. "Is that what you came here to talk about, your job?"

Once the door was no longer between them, Shep felt the full impact of Andrea's magnetism. Immediately he felt a tug of desire, a stirring in his groin. She looked beautiful in a dark gray overcoat. There was a bright green scarf around her neck, and high-heeled black boots on her feet.

"No," he answered truthfully. "But if we get past the animosity between us, I'd like to tell you about it."

"You admit there is animosity between us." She was speaking coldly, acting as though she weren't achingly aware of his handsome features and how appealing he looked with snowflakes in his thick, dark hair.

"Of course I admit it," he said quietly. "Andrea, may I come in?"

"To talk."

"Yes, to talk."

"Nothing else."

"I promise."

He is *Lucas's son,* she told herself. And she *was* curious about his job.

"All right," she conceded, backing up so he could enter. After closing the door, she shed her coat and scarf and hung them in the closet, exposing the stylish business suit she had on under it. "Do you want to take off your jacket?" she asked tonelessly.

"I'll take it off, but I'll keep it with me. I won't be here very long."

"Fine," she said stiffly, marching over to her chair. Moving her purse and the manila envelope to a table, she sat down. "Have a seat if you want," she told him.

"Thanks." Carrying his jacket, he sat on the sofa. He looked around. "There's a lot more room in here without the Christmas tree, isn't there?"

She didn't plan on making small talk with him. Other than finding out about his job, of course. "Get to the point, Shep. Why are you here?"

His eyes met hers. "To get past that animosity we spoke about. Andrea, there's no reason why we can't be friends."

Her expression remained cool and distant. "Do you honestly believe that?"

Silently Shep studied her for a long moment. She wanted honesty? So be it.

"No," he said softly. "I don't believe you and I could ever be just friends."

His candor took Andrea by surprise. It took a second to recover, but then she said, "Wasn't that a rather abrupt about-face? One minute you're talking about friendship, and the next reneging on the idea. I don't know how to take you, Shep. I don't know what to believe or doubt about you."

"You weren't doubtful about me on New Year's Eve."

She flushed. "Maybe not, but everyone's entitled to a moronic mistake now and then."

"That's what it was to you, a mistake?"

"I believe I said '*moronic* mistake.'" She was suddenly too agitated to sit still and got to her feet. "You felt exactly the same, or you never would have apologized. So please don't insult my intelligence by denying it."

Shep, too, stood up, leaving his jacket lying on the couch. "I'm not denying anything, Andrea. At the time, it did seem like a mistake."

"And now it doesn't?" Her voice dripped with sarcasm.

He ignored her tone and calmly nodded. "That's right."

"And I'm supposed to get all thrilled and giddy because you've changed your mind? You must think I'm ten varieties of sap."

Shep's hands itched to touch her. He took a step toward her. "I think nothing of the kind. Your intelligence is as obvious as your beauty."

She had noticed that step he'd taken in her direction and the subtle changes in the air, in his eyes, his stance. His compliment about her intelligence and beauty reinforced her interpretation of those changes.

"Don't come any closer," she told him. "And don't waste your breath on meaningless flattery. As the saying goes, in case it slipped your mind, flattery will get you nowhere."

"Really? What makes you think I want to get somewhere?"

He had taken another step toward her, a very long step. Andrea backed up, but the room was small and she felt a circular table bearing a lamp and a crystal candy dish against her hips.

"That was said much too smoothly," she retorted, hoping she sounded self-assured and in control of her emotions, which definitely was not the case. Her heart was beating hard enough to smother her, and the wilting, will-ing-female sensation in her system was maddening. But this man, as much and as often as she'd told herself that she hated him, radiated something she'd never had to battle before. She couldn't even give it a name, which was infu-riating when it seemed to be devouring her.

"Maybe...maybe you'd better leave now," she stam-mered.

He took the final step that placed him directly in front of her. His dark, smoldering eyes bored into hers. "You do something to me, Andrea. I came here merely seeking friendship. Your driving past me this morning without so much as a smile nagged at me all day. Why shouldn't we be friends, I kept asking myself. We're neighbors and, from the looks of it, we're going to *be* neighbors for some time. Did I want to explain to Dad why you were angry with me? Would you want to explain it? My answer to both ques-tions was no, that neither of us would want Dad to know what took place between us.

"It's a beautiful memory, Andrea, one of the most spe-cial of my life." Shep raised his hand and twined a curl near her ear around his forefinger. He would swear that he hadn't come here for this, and that he'd been totally sin-cere in merely seeking friendship with Andrea, but she was so beautiful and so very, very desirable.

She couldn't tear her eyes from his. He was so close she could smell his clean scent, and his hand near her face, his fingers in her hair, seemed to mesmerize her. If she didn't move or do something, Shep was going to kiss her, and she already knew where kisses led for them.

Shep knew also, which was why he slowly lowered his head and pressed his lips to hers. It was as though all the strength in her body suddenly deserted her, because she slumped against him, weak-kneed and limp. His arms were instantly around her, not only to support her but to savor the stimulation of her body against his, while he deepened the kiss until hoarse little moans came from the bottom of her throat.

Breathing hard, he raised his head to look into her eyes. "You couldn't be angry with me and kiss me like that," he whispered raggedly.

"I guess not," she whispered back, all traces of her former resentment and anger apparently demolished. "But this isn't right, Shep. I've never had an affair and I don't want one now. We hardly know each other. What happened on New Year's Eve *was* a mistake. Maybe it was the champagne, or maybe we were lonely. Whatever, I'm asking you now to stop."

"Stop?" he echoed incredulously. His arousal was straining the seams of his jeans, and she wanted him to stop?

"Yes."

Her eyes contained a plea he couldn't ignore. It was just about the most difficult thing he'd ever forced himself to do, but he simultaneously took a breath, a step back and let go of her.

Andrea laid one hand on the table and brought the other to the base of her throat. "Thank you," she said huskily.

He couldn't stop staring at her. "You know I want you."

"Yes. But let's take it a step at a time. On New Year's, we went a little crazy. At least I did. I don't sleep with men I don't know, Shep. And you regretted it, too."

"It just took me by surprise, Andrea."

Feeling a little steadier, Andrea left the table and sank into her chair. "Let's agree that it took us both by surprise."

Shep realized that she wasn't at all angry with him anymore. She would wave and smile, should they drive past each other again, and maybe she was right about not rushing into an affair.

He sat on the couch again. "I have a job."

Her eyes got big. "So do I! Where are you working?"

"In the hospital's emergency-care department. What about you?"

"At the newspaper. Have you read the *Rocky Ford News*?"

Shep nodded. "Many times. Was that where you were going this morning?"

"My first day on the job."

"Doing what, Andrea?"

That was when she wilted again, only this time it wasn't from passion. Somehow, she managed to keep her trepidation over her own abilities, or lack thereof, from showing on her face, and she answered quite calmly, "Writer and reporter."

"Is that what you did in California?"

Her gaze slid from his. "More or less." Oh, God, what was she going to do about the editorial? If she accomplished nothing else for Saturday's edition, she *had* to write an editorial.

She looked at Shep again, and an idea struck her. "Would you mind seeing your name in the paper?"

"Pardon?"

"I'd like to write about the town's newcomers. Yes," she said, beginning to get excited about the idea. "What brought them here, what they're doing, things like that."

"Andrea, no way would I permit any reporter to explain my reason for returning to Rocky Ford."

"That's it!" she exclaimed. "The article shouldn't be about just any newcomers, but about people who once lived here and came back. Shep, if I keep the article impersonal...I mean, I could skip over your reason for coming back and concentrate on your feelings about being in your hometown again, and about your job, and—" Andrea got up to pace as her imagination took wings "—your high-school years in Rocky Ford and how the town looks to you now. Oh, there are so many things."

She turned to give him an imploring look. "Please say yes. I promise to let you read it before anyone else sees it."

His eyes narrowed slightly. She sounded desperate, which was a little puzzling, but he now knew that she was becoming very important to him. Refusing her request could set their burgeoning relationship back twenty paces, but he didn't want to read about himself in the local newspaper. It was a dilemma, and he wasn't thrilled with it.

"And if I don't like what you've written?" he asked quietly, avoiding a flat-out refusal for the moment.

"I'll change it. Your private life will remain private, you have my word."

His "private life" now revolved around her. How strange. He'd come home devastated over his divorce, and it was no longer important.

Still, he didn't want it mentioned in Andrea's article. Nor did he want to be the focal point of the area's entire population until something else came along to whet their appetite for gossip. And if he remembered correctly, very few of the town's residents didn't read Kathleen Osterman's newspaper. Bottom line—he neither liked Andrea's idea nor wanted to be a part of it.

"Tell you what," he said, again hedging against an all-out refusal. "Give me a little time to think about it, and maybe we can work something out."

"Shep, there is no time. I need this article for Saturday's edition."

The frantic edge on her voice caused Shep's heart to sink. They had made such great headway this evening, and he didn't want to ruin it. But he simply could not have his name and story in the paper, however discreetly written.

"This has to be a new project, am I right?" he asked.

Andrea felt the excitement of her idea fading away. If he was going to agree, he would already have done it. "You know it is," she said quietly. "You don't want to do it, do you?"

Shep got up from the couch and walked over to her. She didn't flinch or draw away when he tipped her chin and looked into her eyes. "Do you have any idea how tough it is for me to refuse to do something that seems so important to you?" he asked softly.

"But you're averse to the project and you have to say no, don't you?"

"Does that make you angry?"

Could she ever be truly angry with him again? He'd broken through her self-protective barrier against his charm this evening, and she doubted her ability to resurrect it. She sighed heavily. "I'm not angry."

"Andrea, thank you," he whispered, pulling her into his arms. Cradling her head on his chest, he held her. The inevitable began occurring, but he had agreed—he *had* agreed, hadn't he?—to take their relationship one step at a time, so he didn't act upon his racing pulse and erotic thoughts.

After a few moments, she moved away from him. "I have work to do. Don't take this wrong, but I really must ask you to leave."

He studied her pretty face, looking for signs of deception. There were none. She was telling him the truth. She had work to do and needed to be alone.

He picked up his jacket. "Will you have dinner with me tomorrow night?"

"I . . . I don't know. Do our shifts coincide?"

"I leave for work at ten-thirty. My shift runs from 11:00 p.m. to 7:00 a.m. I was coming home from my first night on the job when we passed on the road this morning."

"You work at night?" There was surprise in her expression.

He grinned a little. "It was the only opening. It's a job, Andrea, and I'm glad to have it."

"But you're a specialist."

"Dad's words, almost exactly. Right now, emergency care is fine. Getting back to dinner tomorrow—"

She broke in. "It depends on how much I accomplish here tonight and tomorrow at the office. Can we leave it open for now?"

"Sure, no problem." Putting on his jacket, he walked to the door. Andrea followed, and just before he turned the knob to leave, he tipped her chin again and tenderly kissed her lips.

Her breath caught in her throat. How easy—and wonderful—it would be to ask him to stay. He had hours before his shift began. They could make love again and again. . . .

She broke the kiss and attempted a smile. "Drive carefully tonight. The roads were already getting clogged with snow when I came home."

He nodded. "See you tomorrow."

He left her house feeling good and trudged through the heavy snowfall back to his dad's house barely noticing the cold.

Seven

Andrea still thought her idea for a series of articles on Rocky Ford residents who had left for one reason or another and then returned was a good one. But she had no place to start. Shep, having become a doctor during his absence, would have made an interesting initial article, and she was disappointed over his refusal to participate.

But she also understood it. A need for privacy was something she understood very well, and she couldn't fault Shep for guarding his.

Still, his refusal had put her back to square one as far as a nice series of human-interest articles went. Scratch that idea for the next edition, she told herself, but there was still the editorial to get through. Kathleen hadn't told her to do the paper's customary editorials in her absence, but then Kathleen hadn't been especially specific about anything. And maybe all Kathleen wanted from her was to be on hand should an event occur in the area that required someone with a journalistic background to report.

But Andrea's experience was so limited. A degree in journalism, good grades and some published articles in the college paper did not a reporter make. She felt she was a good writer, but accurately critiquing one's own work was impossible. Whatever, she should probably just count herself lucky and stop trying to second-guess Kathleen's decision to hire her.

What she could not trivialize or overlook, however, was the opportunity Kathleen had handed her. She had to justify Kathleen's faith in her, which meant, in Andrea's estimation, at least one good article with her byline in each edition of the paper. Or at least an acceptable editorial.

While she made and ate a light supper, then showered and got into her nightclothes, she racked her brain about that editorial.

That wasn't altogether true. Entwined with her excitement and worry about her job were thoughts of Shep. His kiss at the door had been sweet; the first one had been wildly passionate. She had enjoyed both.

There was no avoiding her feelings for Shep, however foolish they were. The long and the short of it was that she had fallen in love with him at first sight, and even the emotional pain he'd inflicted on New Year's Eve hadn't destroyed that love. It didn't make her happy, because for all she knew he could still be in love with his ex-wife. His physical attraction for *her* didn't mean much in the long run. He was very male and macho, and undoubtedly not accustomed to living a celibate life. If she wasn't in the picture, depressing as the thought was, another woman would be.

So she dare not make too much of Shep's attentions. And her decision against the two of them conducting an affair was a wise one. At least she'd done something right in that regard.

Andrea worked until midnight, and although she wasn't thrilled with the editorial she'd written, it was something to turn in. And maybe it wasn't so bad for a first effort, she told herself as she wearily crawled into bed.

Her final thoughts before sleep were about Kathleen. If she wasn't too heavily sedated in preparation for surgery tomorrow, she was probably worrying about her newspaper.

Andrea said a prayer for Kathleen's recovery, then closed her eyes. Her first day as a newswoman was over.

Andrea was shocked when she looked out the window in the morning. It was still snowing, and the fresh snow on her driveway was at least three feet deep. Yanking on a fleecy gray sweat suit, her boots and heavy jacket, she trudged through the deep snow to the street. It wasn't plowed!

Frantically she raced back to the house and picked up the phone. There was no dial tone.

"Oh, my Lord," she whispered. She knew she had electricity, because she'd turned on several lights while getting up, but for how long? Even if she managed to shovel out her long driveway, she couldn't go anywhere until the snowplows cleared the streets. And she couldn't even phone the paper to let them know how stranded she was.

Someone pounded on her back door. "Andrea?"

It was Lucas. Hurriedly Andrea unlocked and opened the door. "Lucas, this is terrible. My phone isn't working. Is yours?"

"No, and I knew you'd be scared. I've seen this kind of weather before, and you haven't. The town's only got a couple of plows, and they're probably working like crazy to keep the main thoroughfares clear. They might not get out this way for hours, maybe not even today."

"Is Shep home?"

"Not yet, and I doubt if he will be until the roads are plowed."

Andrea dropped onto a chair. "I *have* to get to work, Lucas." She sounded panicked.

"Shep told me about your job. You have to stop worrying, honey. We're not the only ones stranded at home or, like Shep, stuck at their jobs because of the snow. The people who own four-wheelers are probably getting around, but the rest of us are just going to have to stay put and wait for the plows." Lucas laid his gloved hands on the sink counter and looked out the window. "It's coming down faster than the plows can work. And according to the forecast I heard on the radio, there's no end in sight."

Andrea was aghast. "You mean this could go on for days?"

Lucas turned. "It could. How's your food supply?"

"I have plenty of food. What about you?"

"No problem there. I only hope the electricity doesn't go off. Could get a mite uncomfortable without our furnaces functioning."

Andrea's shoulders slumped. It was too far to walk to the newspaper office in so much snow, and she couldn't even call in. Oh, the phones just had to be working now! Jumping up, she went to the kitchen extension and prayed for a dial tone.

"It's still dead," she told Lucas. "Why would the phones be affected by snow?"

"It's the telephone lines, honey. They get weighted down and snap sometimes. Real cold temperatures can do it, too. I would imagine the maintenance crews are out in full force."

"Well, this is just great," Andrea said disgustedly. "I had no idea this part of Montana got so much snow."

"It's rare, honey. I remember other winters this bad, but we've had pretty mild weather for years now."

"Wonderful," Andrea muttered. She took off her jacket, draped it over the back of a chair, then started preparing a pot of coffee. "Take off your jacket," she said to Lucas over her shoulder. "Have you had breakfast?"

"I was waiting for Shep. But I'm going to refuse your invitation, honey. I'm going to hike down to old Mrs. Shank's place and make sure she's all right."

"Mrs. Shank?"

"She lives about a mile down the road. Almost ninety years old and pretty spry for her age. But she doesn't have any family in the area, and I check on her every so often."

Andrea frowned. "That's very good of you, Lucas, but should you be walking a mile in this weather?"

Lucas grinned. "What do you think I am, an old man?"

"Of course you're not old, but..."

Lucas's grin turned into a laugh. "Don't worry, I'll be just fine." He went to the door. "Oh, if Shep should happen to get through and you see him, tell him where I went, okay?"

"I'll tell him." Andrea held the door open while Lucas went through it. "Be careful, Lucas."

"I'm always careful, honey. See you later."

Andrea watched him vanish in the dense snowfall, then sighed and closed the door. This was a fine kettle of fish. Her second day on a new job, and she couldn't even get to it. Had Sally and the others made it to work?

After turning on the radio to keep up with the weather reports, she ate some toast with her first cup of coffee, then in the next hour, finished the pot while pacing and worrying. Every few minutes, she tried the phone again, and every few minutes her frustration went deeper. She couldn't even call the hospital in Missoula to check on Kathleen's postsurgery condition, which she had planned on doing. She couldn't do *anything*, dammit. She was stranded in her own home, completely out of touch with the rest of the world.

And every time she got near a window and looked out, her spirits dropped another notch. The snow just kept falling, and falling. And piling up, deeper and deeper.

She nearly jumped out of her skin when a fist pounded on her front door. Running to it, she called, "Who is it?"

"Shep."

She yanked the door open. He was covered with snow and looked half-frozen. "What in the world...? How did you get here?"

"A male nurse at the hospital has a snowmobile. He gave me a ride home. Do you happen to know where Dad might be? He isn't home."

"He said he was going to check on Mrs. Shank. You look frozen to death. Take off that jacket and stand over the furnace vent. You need to warm up."

"He *walked* to the Shank home?"

"I told him he shouldn't, but he went anyway."

"He shouldn't be out in this, Andrea. It's bad, really bad. And it's getting worse by the hour. I think I'd better go and make sure he's all right."

Just then the phone rang. "It's working!" Andrea exclaimed, dashing to answer it. "Hello?"

"Andrea, it's me, Lucas. I'm at Mrs. Shank's house, and everything's fine."

Before Andrea could say one word, the line went dead. "No!" she cried. "Not again!"

Shep all but ran to her side. "What's wrong?"

"The phone went dead again. It was your dad. He said he's with Mrs. Shank and everything is fine. But I didn't get to say a word to him." With a fitful sigh, she put the phone down. "I've never been through anything like this. It's horrible."

"It's not as bad as an earthquake. You must have lived through a couple of those in California." Shep shed his gloves, scarf and jacket. "Where should I put these? They're wet."

"I'll hang them over a chair to dry." Andrea noticed the blotchy dampness of his jeans. "Better get out of those, too."

Shep grinned. Now that he knew his dad was safe and sound, this was kind of fun. "Anything you say, Andrea." Without a qualm, he unbuttoned and unzipped his jeans and stepped out of them.

"I didn't mean in here," she exclaimed, looking everywhere but at his briefs. "Hang them on another chair. Then make yourself useful and build a fire in the fireplace while I get you a blanket."

Chuckling, Shep strolled into the living room and started building that fire. He could hear the radio in the kitchen and stopped to listen.

"The highway patrol has issued an advisory for the Gates, Claryville and Rocky Ford areas. Roads are all but impassable and very dangerous. So stay at home, folks. Or stay wherever you are. The U.S. Weather Bureau predicts at least one more day of continuous snow."

Andrea had also heard the broadcast. Walking into the living room with a blanket and a downcast expression, she spoke disgustedly. "Another day of this, and the snow will be up to our chimneys."

Shep laughed. "It won't be that bad, honey. You might as well relax and enjoy it."

She handed him the blanket. "Enjoy being trapped? Obviously, my idea of pleasure and yours are miles apart."

Wrapping the blanket around his waist and tucking it together so it would stay put, he smiled wickedly, and Andrea didn't miss the devilish twinkle in his eyes, either. "Oh, I don't think our individual conceptions of pleasure are that far apart," he said.

She flushed. "We are talking about two separate things, and you know it. Please skip the innuendo, if you don't mind. I'm really not in the mood for it."

Andrea had barely finished her final sentence when the radio and lights went off. "Oh, no," she wailed. "Not the power, too."

Shep could tell that she wasn't just complaining; she was genuinely alarmed. He'd grown up with snow and she had not, and while he'd seen only a few storms of this caliber himself, Andrea had never seen even one.

He went to her, put his arms around her and brought her head to his shirtfront. "Don't be frightened," he said soothingly. "I won't leave you here alone."

"Oh, Shep," she sighed. "I feel so helpless. Now we won't even have heat."

"We have the fireplace, and there's plenty of wood. If you have food, we'll make it just fine."

"There's lots of food."

"Have you checked your faucets?"

She reared her head back from his chest to see his face. "My faucets?" she repeated, mystified.

"Water pipes freeze in this kind of weather. Dad has every exposed pipe wrapped with insulation. Do you?"

"I don't know," she wailed, and tore free of his embrace to run to the kitchen to turn on a faucet. A relief of enormous proportions weakened her knees; there was no problem with the water. "It's working," she told Shep, who had followed on her heels.

"To play it safe, leave a small stream running in here and in the bathroom sink."

"Really? Wouldn't that be wasting a lot of water?"

"Sometimes it's necessary. Here, I'll adjust it to minimize the waste." He took her place at the sink and turned the faucet handle until just a tiny stream of water flowed from the tap. "That'll keep the water moving in the pipes and prevent freezing," he told her.

"Well, you obviously know more about this than I do," she said with a forlorn sigh.

"I'll take care of the bathroom fixtures. Go and sit by the fire. It's already starting to cool down in here."

He was right. Without the furnace blasting warm air through the vents, the house was getting cool. The atmosphere was also rather gray without the lights on.

While Shep left the kitchen for the bathroom, Andrea tried the phone again. Shaking her head, she put down the lifeless instrument, then went to the living room and sat on the rug in front of the fire. Drawing her knees up, she wrapped her arms around them and stared into the flames. *Thank goodness the house has a fireplace,* she thought, although she was beginning to realize that most of the heat from the fire was going up the chimney. It was going to get very cold without the furnace, especially tonight.

Shep came in and sat next to her. "How long do you think the electricity will be off?" she asked without looking at him.

He didn't want to worry her more than she already was. "Probably not long."

She turned her head to see him. "You're just saying that to make me feel better."

His ploy hadn't worked. She was too perceptive to be consoled by a comment about a subject he couldn't possibly have accurate answers for.

She faced the fire again. "Have you seen a storm this bad before?"

"A couple of times."

"What did you do? I mean, how did you and Lucas stay warm?"

"The worst storm was when I was about five or six. We had no utilities for two days, if I'm remembering it right. My mother was alive then. She and Dad took me in their bed, and we bundled up together until the heat came on. I remember it as fun, Andrea. Mother read stories to me and made up some of her own to keep me entertained. When we got hungry, either her or Dad would run to the kitchen and make sandwiches. Dad had one of those propane camp stoves, and he heated soup and made tea and coffee on it."

Andrea looked at him again. "That sounds like a lovely memory."

"I haven't thought of it in years, but you're right, it's a very special memory." Shep paused a moment, then added softly, "Mother died a few years later."

"I'm sorry. You were so young. You must have been devastated."

"I don't remember much about it, to tell the truth. Blocked it out, I suppose. Anyway, Dad was always there, and I adjusted, as kids do."

"You were fortunate to have your father," Andrea murmured.

Shep sent her a curious glance. "Don't you have yours? I mean, I know your mother passed away last year, but what about your father?"

"He . . . he and Mother divorced when I was just a baby. I don't remember him," Andrea finally managed to say.

"You mean he vanished from your life just because your parents divorced? What the hell kind of guy was he?" Shep sounded angry.

This conversation was going in a direction that made Andrea very uncomfortable. She got to her feet. "I'm going to check the phone again. Would you lay another log on the fire, please?"

She hurried into the kitchen and picked up the phone. It was still dead, but she might not have heard a dial tone over the loud beating of her heart anyway. Lucas had always been there for Shep, and where had her father been? Hiding in a little town in Montana, not giving a hang about his daughter in California. Charlie *couldn't* be the nice guy Lucas had proclaimed him to be. Nice guys didn't turn their backs on their children.

The chill settling upon the house penetrated Andrea's clothing. Shivering, she went to her bedroom for two more blankets, then went to the living room, gave one to Shep and draped the other around her shoulders. Sitting cross-legged, she held her hands out to the fire.

"Thanks," he said.

"It's getting colder in here."

"And it's going to get even colder, Andrea." He grinned at her. "We might have to bundle together in bed to survive the night."

Her cheeks got pink, but she ignored his remark and asked instead, "Aren't you planning on going to work tonight?"

"I'd go if I could get there."

"You didn't ask your pal with the snowmobile to pick you up tonight?"

"When I left the hospital this morning, the phones were still working. All I knew was that the roads were too clogged to use my car, so I bummed a ride home. But it never occurred to me that I wouldn't be able to call Jerry later today. Pretty poor planning on my part."

Andrea sighed. "Well, you could hardly predict what the day was going to bring. Maybe Jerry will think to come and get you without a call."

"Possibly," Shep concurred.

"In that case, shouldn't you be sleeping? You worked all last night, and if you work again tonight without sleeping today, you're going to be very tired."

"I'll be fine. Probably catch a nap later."

And just like that, they ran out of small talk. Andrea tugged the blanket around her shoulders tighter, trying desperately to think of something to say. Shep was hunched under his own blanket, but they were sitting no more than six inches apart because of the modest size of the fireplace.

"Uh...maybe your jeans are dry by now," she stammered.

He gave her a tongue-in-cheek look. "Want me to put my pants on, eh?"

"Only for your own comfort."

She sounded a little churlish, making Shep chuckle to himself. This togetherness business was getting to her, and the day was still young. By the time this storm was over, they would either be lovers again or enemies. He was going to do his level best to accomplish the former. Opportunities like this one didn't come along every day, and he couldn't see any sensible reason for them to maintain an arms-length relationship. And it wasn't just sex for him, either. Andrea became more important to him every time he saw her, and even when he wasn't with her she was uppermost in his thoughts. Now, whether or not his feelings were serious enough to start thinking about a commingled future was another matter entirely. He certainly wasn't enchanted with the idea of marriage, not after the ruinous fall and crash of his first attempt at the institution.

But they were both adults, and Andrea had already proved how strongly attracted she was to him. New Year's Eve had not been a fluke. Sitting with her right this minute, he could sense how tautly she was strung simply because they were alone and he was partially undressed.

He thought of candidly speaking his thoughts. *Why don't we stop pretending we're only acquaintances and go to bed together, the way we both want to do?*

But of course he couldn't do that. Andrea was a woman that needed subtle wooing, and didn't he himself prefer romance over crudity?

At any rate, the tension was mounting between them. If the plows didn't come, and if the electricity and phones stayed off, and if it kept snowing and everything remained the same, they would be sharing the same bed tonight.

He would bet on it.

Eight

Charlie Fanon had left the Closed sign in his coffee-shop window that morning; no one would be coming in on a day like this.

Last night, he'd gone outside and sniffed the freezing air; the snow coming down and the smell of the storm told him what he'd wanted to know. He'd gone into his toolshed for the two kerosene space heaters he owned and also brought out his propane camp stove. He then spent the evening cleaning all three items, wiping away dust and making sure they worked since he hadn't used them in some time.

He had awakened at his usual time this morning, 5:00 a.m., and immediately checked the weather. Not particularly thrilled with the accuracy of his sensory perception last night about the intensity and duration of the storm, he next checked the utilities. Everything was working, but he couldn't help wondering for how long.

He made himself some breakfast and listened to the radio while he ate. There was no good news: roads were impassable, schools were closed, people were advised to venture outdoors only for an emergency, and so on and so on.

The phone rang while he was doing the few dishes he'd used. He picked up the kitchen extension. "Charlie Fanon."

"Dad, we're snowed in."

It was Serena, Charlie's daughter. "Everyone is, honey. Is Trav with you?"

Trav was Serena's husband. "Yes, thank goodness."

Serena and Trav's house was on beautiful ground fronting Access Creek, but Trav's businesses kept him on the road a lot. Charlie was relieved that Serena wasn't alone way out there where they lived.

"Serena, do you and Trav have space heaters that function on something other than electricity?"

"We have two fireplaces and plenty of wood, Dad."

"Yes, but I want you to check with Trav about the heaters. And if you have a propane camp stove, dig it out. I'm surprised the utilities haven't already gone out."

Charlie could hear his daughter talking to her husband. "Do we have any space heaters or a propane camp stove?"

Trav came on the line. "Charlie, if the utilities go, Serena and I will move into the motor home. It's self-contained, with a propane furnace and battery-powered electricity. With care, we could get by for three or four days."

"That's right," Charlie exclaimed. "I forgot about your motor home."

"Here, I'm giving you back to Serena. Take care, Charlie."

The phone was passed. "Dad, I called to find out if *you* were all right. How are you fixed for groceries? Trav could try and get through with his four-wheeler if you need anything."

"Tell Trav to stay home and take care of you two. I have everything I need, honey, and neither of you are to spend the day worrying about me. That's an order."

Serena laughed, as Charlie had known she would. He only issued orders in jest, and the whole family knew it.

"All right, Dad. But if you decide you need something later on, be sure and call."

Charlie said he would just to ease Serena's concerns about him. But he'd been through several of this type of storm during his years in Montana, and he very strongly expected the utilities to go any minute.

He had no more than hung up from Serena's call when the phone rang again. This time it was Lola.

"Charlie, isn't this storm a humdinger?"

"Sure is, honey. Are you and Duke snowed in?"

Duke and Lola owned and lived on the immense Sheridan ranch some thirty miles from town. But Charlie had every faith in Duke's ability to weather any kind of storm. His only concern about the Sheridans lay with Lola, who was pregnant.

"Duke and his men are plowing snow and feeding the cattle," Lola said. "The reason I called was to make sure you were okay."

"I'm fine. Are you?"

"Me, personally? Yes, Charlie, I'm healthy as a horse. Don't worry, Duke's keeping a very close eye on me."

"I knew he would be, but you can't blame me for worrying about you just a little. Many of the roads are closed, Lola, and if a problem should develop—"

"Duke would get me to the hospital if he had to carry me on his back. Either that or deliver the baby himself." Lola chuckled. "He said it couldn't be much different than delivering a foal or a calf. He was kidding, of course."

"Delivering the baby wouldn't be the problem, honey. It's the fact that it would be coming sooner than it should."

"I know, Charlie, and I'm being especially cautious right now. Duke won't even let me stick my head out the door."

"Good for him."

"Have you talked to Serena or Candace?"

"Serena called a few minutes ago."

"Then you'll probably be hearing from Candace next. For my own peace of mind, I need to make contact with the family, so I'll call Serena first, then Candace. If you need anything, Charlie, be sure and call on the Sheridans. There isn't a storm bad enough that could keep Duke from rushing to your aid. However clogged the roads are, he would get to town, I guarantee it."

"I believe he would, honey. Thanks for the call."

Affection for his family brought a smile to Charlie's lips as he put down the phone. He knew when it rang again a few minutes later that it would be Candace on the line.

"Hello, Candace," he said.

She laughed. "How did you know it was me?"

"Because Serena and Lola have already called. Let me put your mind to rest right up front, honey. I'm fine. I have plenty of food, I'm not ill and I have a family that loves me. What more could a man want?" He chuckled a little. "But I'm glad you called. Are you and Burke all right? And how's my grandson doing?"

"We're all well and happy... in spite of the worst storm I've ever seen." Candace had been born and raised in South Carolina, and she had never seen snow like this. "Ronnie insisted on following Burke down to the barn to check on the animals, and you would have laughed if you'd seen how I bundled him up. You can't see anything but his eyes. Burke put him on the sled and pulled him to the barn. The snow is deeper than Ronnie is tall."

"He and Burke are great pals, aren't they?"

"Yes, they are. Charlie, there's something Burke and I want to talk to you about. After this awful storm is over, of course."

"Burke would like to adopt Ronnie," Charlie said quietly.

Candace was silent a moment, then spoke quietly, too. "We talked it over, Charlie, and if you have the slightest objection..."

Ronnie's birth father was Charlie's son, Ron, who had been killed in the military. Charlie adored his grandson, but he had great affection for Burke Mallory, Candace's second husband, as well.

"I think it's a great idea, Candy. A sensible idea. Tell Burke he has my blessing."

"Oh, Charlie, you're the best," Candace said with a catch in her voice.

"So are you, honey, and so is Burke. Tell him hello when he comes in, and give Ronnie a big hug for me."

"I will, Charlie. Well, I just wanted to make sure you were all right. Call if you need anything. Burke and I would find a way to get it to you, I promise."

Charlie smiled. Burke, Candace and Ronnie lived eighty miles away, but he knew Candace was sincere in her promise to help, should he need anything.

"Goodbye, honey." He put the phone down and went to the sink to finish the dishes.

There were some folks right here in town that he should check on himself, he thought while drying his hands. Returning to the phone, he picked it up and realized it was dead.

So it begins, he thought while wandering into the coffee shop, which was located in the front portion of his house. Sipping coffee, he watched the hard snowfall through the large windows facing the street. No one was out and about. Occasionally a four-wheeler with chains on its tires lumbered and clanked by, but that was about it.

A debilitating loneliness struck Charlie suddenly and without warning. His body reacted physically to the destructive emotion with an overfast heartbeat and a feeling of breathlessness.

"You're a very fortunate man," he told himself out loud. "Don't start feeling sorry for yourself because you're alone."

But he hated living alone. *Oh, for just one day when the kids were young and running in and out of the house, full of life and sweet, so very, very sweet.*

Now he lived on memories, and that wasn't good for anyone. He had lived alone before, of course. Ron had joined the army and had been living on the East Coast, Lola had been traveling all over the globe and Serena had been in college, then law school.

But Charlie had been younger then, and he'd known his kids would come home again, maybe one at a time, maybe all together.

Now he had no such solace to fall back on. Charlie's son was dead, and his girls were married with homes of their own. He was getting old and he was alone.

"You damned wimp," he muttered at himself, angry that he would feel such intense self-pity. And Charlie didn't get angry easily or often. But this was ridiculous. If he didn't want to live alone, there were ways around it. He could take in boarders, for instance, fill all those empty bedrooms and hire a cook and housekeeper. He could have the old house jumping with activity, if that was what he wanted.

Or... he could marry again. Yes, he thought with a reviving spirit, why not marry again? He'd only been married once, and that had happened a very long time ago. There were dozens of widows in the immediate area, ladies who were probably as lonely as he was.

But just not any widow lady would do. He would want someone... jolly. Yes, a jolly woman who laughed and kidded and didn't spend every minute of every day complaining about her aches and pains. She wouldn't have to be a beauty. Heck, he'd lost his own looks years ago, and beauty was only skin-deep anyway.

His eyes narrowed as he mentally visualized the women he knew, one by one. And then, for some reason, he thought of Sandra, his ex-wife. She'd been a beauty, no doubt about it.

But she'd also had a heart like ice and had left him and their two small children without a backward glance. When Ron and Serena were old enough to ask about their mother, he'd told them she was dead. To him, it had seemed kinder to tell them that than the truth, that she simply hadn't wanted them and that she had walked out of their lives, completely vanished and had never once tried to see her babies.

He had left California and moved to Montana. Ron and Serena had grown up in Rocky Ford. Lola had come to live with them when she was nine years old, after the death of her parents. Her father had been Charlie's only brother, and Charlie hadn't been able to bear the thought of little Lola growing up without family. She had become as dear to him as his own children, and he still thought of her as one of his kids.

Charlie was still deep in the past when the lights went out. He sat there for a while, then sighed, got up and went to get his space heaters. Bringing them into the coffee shop, he closed the door that connected the shop and living quarters of his house.

The two heaters were efficient, and the coffee shop remained snug and warm.

And Charlie sat there, sipped coffee, watched the storm and thought about life in general and his own in particular.

After a while, he reached a very sad conclusion: he was no longer a happy man.

So... was he going to do something about it or wallow in self-pity for the rest of his days?

He took a deep breath. By damn, he was *not* going to wallow again. He'd figure out something to make life worthwhile again, or his name wasn't Charlie Fanon.

And that was a vow.

By afternoon, the storm had changed. The temperature was dropping, the falling snow had become much smaller flakes and a strong north wind was blowing. Andrea and Shep kept feeding the fire in the fireplace, but it was a feeble heat and the house kept getting colder.

When Shep put on his jeans and jacket and said he was going to check on his dad's house, Andrea felt a little panicky. "But you're coming back, aren't you?" she asked.

Shep wrapped one of the blankets he'd been using around her shoulders, topping the one she was already wearing. "I'll be back," he told her. Flirtatiously he touched the tip of her nose and grinned. "Your nose is cold. You need a nose mitten."

She laughed and held her hand over her nose to warm it up. Then she followed him to the back door. "Don't get lost. It's blowing so much snow around, there's zero visibility out there. I can't even see the fence from here.''

"Don't worry. I'll turn on my radar and navigate by instrument.''

His silly comment and teasing tone made her laugh again. But after he'd vanished into the storm, her laughter died. Shivering, she snuggled deeper into her blankets and returned to the fire.

Without Shep in the house, the fury of the storm seemed louder and more threatening. How long would he be gone? Fifteen minutes should do it, she thought hopefully. After all, what was there to check? She would bet anything that Lucas's home was as winterized as he'd been able to make it. Other than greenhorns like herself, the residents of Rocky Ford knew what to do to survive weather like this. Why, she hadn't even known to let the faucets run a stream of water to prevent frozen pipes. Shep had told her that precaution didn't always work—should the electricity stay off for an extended period and the temperature inside approach the awful cold outside, for example—but it was working so far. To be on the safe side, she had filled several large containers with water, for if the pipes froze, the final working utility would be useless.

My, one felt helpless without electricity and a phone, Andrea thought, marveling how she'd always taken such comforts for granted. Push a button, and there was light. Turn up the thermostat, and warmth flowed from the furnace vents. Pick up the phone, and talk to someone on the other side of the world. Hungry? Just turn on the stove and cook something to eat.

How had the pioneers survived Rocky Mountain winters?

Many of them *hadn't* survived, she recalled from history books. And small wonder, she thought with another bout of the shivers.

While Andrea was huddling in her blankets as close to the fire as was safe, Shep was turning on faucets in Lucas's house. Obviously, his dad had intended to return home immediately after checking on Mrs. Shank. Otherwise, the faucets would already be running a thin stream of water.

He tried Lucas's phone in vain, then went to his bedroom, stripped down and put on a pair of long johns, wool pants, a turtleneck sweater and a flannel shirt over that. He didn't own the kind of jacket one needed in weather like this, but Lucas had several, and Shep went to his father's room and got one of them. He also located a wool stocking cap, scarf and mittens. He'd damned near frozen his ears and buns off during the short hike from Andrea's house to Lucas's, but he wasn't going to freeze going back.

Glancing at himself in a mirror, he couldn't hold back a laugh: he looked like a stuffed sausage.

He was headed out the door when he remembered Lucas's camp stove. Did he still have it? Did it still work?

It could only be in one place, if it existed at all . . . in Lucas's storage room on the back of the house. Shep spotted it only seconds after entering the cramped little room. Elated, he checked the propane canister and read the date on it: it was almost new.

"Great," he said under his breath, taking stove and canister with him. Just before leaving, he remembered one more thing: the bottle of brandy Lucas kept in a cabinet for medicinal purposes.

Tucking the bottle into a pocket of his jacket, he finally left the house. "My God, it's worse," he muttered as the freezing wind buffeted his face with snow pellets.

He walked into Andrea's kitchen without knocking. "It's me," he called out.

Andrea sighed with relief. She hadn't liked being alone and was so glad Shep was back she felt like kissing him. Getting to her feet, she hastened to the kitchen.

Then she laughed. "What on earth have you got on?"

He grinned at her. "Everything warm I could find in the house. And please take note of this." He pointed at the propane stove on the counter. "And this." He pulled the bottle of brandy from his pocket. "How about a hot cup of coffee laced with brandy?"

"Sounds wonderful. But the only coffeepot I have works on electricity."

"Then we'll make camp coffee."

"Oh?"

Shep had been taking off his stocking cap, mittens and jacket. Laying them on a chair, he asked for a pan. Andrea got one from a cupboard, and Shep filled it about half full of water. Then he lifted the top of the little stove and lit a burner, upon which he placed the pan of water.

"Coffee grounds?" he asked.

"Right here." Andrea put a can of coffee in his hand. "Can you light another burner?"

"Sure can."

"I'd like to heat some soup."

While they ate hot soup and cold beef sandwiches, the smell of the boiling coffee permeated the room.

Finally Shep pronounced it ready. He fixed two mugs of coffee and brandy and handed her one. "Now, let's go sit by the fire and get cozy."

From the look in his eyes, "getting cozy" had a multitude of meanings. She smiled. Her feelings for him had compounded a hundredfold today. She not only loved him, but he was her rescuer, her savior. Yes, she would definitely "get cozy" with him and not worry about such an unimportant word as *affair,* either.

They were just settling down when the unmistakable sound of a snowmobile reached their ears. Holding their mugs of coffee and brandy, they looked at each other as the engine noise got louder and closer. They heard the machine stop in front of Lucas's house.

"I'm sure that's Jerry," Shep said. He gave Andrea a placating look and went to open her front door. Andrea saw Shep step outside and heard him shout, "Jerry."

A few moments later, the young man was standing on Andrea's stoop.

"What's up, Jerry?" Andrea listened intently.

"Dr. Wilde, I've been transporting doctors and nurses to and from the hospital all day. Even so, some can't be reached. They're short on staff and sent me for you. Can you come in early?"

"Like right now?" Shep said dryly.

"Yes, sir."

Shep hesitated a moment, then nodded. "I'll get my jacket. Do you want to come inside?"

"I'll wait with my machine. If I get too warm, I'll start sweating in this outfit."

"All right. I'll only be a few minutes." Shep closed the door and gave Andrea an apologetic look. "Sorry, but I have to go."

"Of course you do," she murmured quietly, though her heart was in her throat. He would be gone all night. She would be alone in the coldest, darkest night of her life.

Shep went to the kitchen and returned heaving on his jacket. Andrea was standing, and he walked over and put his arms around her. "The electricity could come back on at any time," he said softly. "Try not to worry. And if the phones start working, I'll call."

Then he kissed her. Feeling the sting of tears in her nose and eyes, she clung to his bulky body and kissed him back with all the love in her heart and soul. She couldn't pretend with him anymore. She couldn't be angry because he'd hurt her on New Year's Eve, or hold back her affection because he might still care for his ex-wife. Nature's fury made everything seem different, altering priorities, trivializing today what had been of the utmost urgency yesterday.

Her emotional response nearly tore Shep apart. Raising his head, he studied the depths of her beautiful eyes. "I wish I didn't have to leave," he said raggedly.

"I wish it more," she whispered.

"Andrea, it's getting dark. Do you have candles and a flashlight?"

"Yes, both."

"If the power's off all night, it's going to get very cold in here. Pile all the blankets you have on the bed and stay under them."

"Shep, how can the hospital function without power?"

"It has its own generators for just this sort of emergency."

"Oh" was all she said.

They could hear Jerry revving the engine of his snowmobile.

"I have to go," Shep said. He kissed her again, walked to the door, then paused to say, "If there's any chance of getting back here before tomorrow, I'll take it. I don't like the idea of your being here by yourself."

Mutely she nodded. But she knew if things remained as they were, he might not be back for days. "Be careful, Shep."

"You, too." He opened the door and was gone.

She watched from a window and saw him get on the machine behind Jerry. It roared away, and once again only the howling wind broke the silence.

Returning to the fireplace, she laid several chunks of wood on the grate. Her supply was getting low, she noticed with a heavy sigh. She would have to save what was left for morning, which meant going to bed very soon now.

Retrieving her mug of coffee and brandy, which had already cooled down, she took a swallow. Her thoughts rambled from Shep to Charlie. If there was any way for her to get to Charlie's house right now, she would go to see him.

How absolutely ludicrous it was that she hadn't done it before this. Getting up, she went to her bookcase and brought her Fanon notebook back to the fire. Slowly she thumbed through the pages and read her own notes and the articles she had clipped from the newspaper and saved.

The fire was dying again, and darkness was falling. Taking her blankets, Andrea laid her notebook on a table, got her flashlight from a drawer in the kitchen and went to her bedroom.

Weighted down with quilts and blankets, she lay in the dark and listened to the storm for hours. She had never felt more alone in her life.

Indeed, she would not easily forget this winter.

Nine

When Shep arrived at the hospital, he and one other doctor, Peter Freeman, G.P., were the only physicians in attendance. They talked while Shep changed from his own clothes into a standard green hospital uniform.

"I've been able to stay in touch with doctors Caldwell and Peterson by cell phone," Dr. Freeman said, touching the cellular telephone on his belt. "Partially in touch, that is. Very poor reception because of the storm, very poor. But they both have serious cases in ICU, and I've been trying to follow their instructions. You're not a trauma-care specialist, are you?"

"No," Shep said. "My only emergency-room experience was during training."

"Well, we're grossly understaffed, and those of us who are here are all going far beyond our normal duties. Just pray we don't have someone come in with symptoms we can't handle. The portable X ray works on our generators, but the large, stationary machine is off-line."

Shep already knew the hospital didn't have a CAT scan or an MRI machine, extremely costly equipment that the small hospital couldn't afford. Patients requiring tests of that nature were normally transported to Missoula's excellent medical facilities. But transporting anyone that distance in this weather—especially someone seriously ill or injured—was next to impossible.

"Hell of a storm," Peter said, starting to walk away. "Page me if something happens you can't handle alone."

"Will do," Shep called after him. Frowning in concern for the town, so helpless without utilities and freedom of movement, he scrubbed at the sink.

Leaving the locker room, he discovered that he had only one nurse—Helen Grant—to rely on. She was not only seeing to two patients in curtained-off areas, but she was also acting as the admitting receptionist. She looked harried and wasted no time in small talk.

"Number two has frostbite and number four has flu symptoms," she told him, referring to the bed numbers behind the curtains. "Their charts are on the counter. I have three people waiting in reception. I can't begin to guess how they're managing to get here. Call me if you need assistance." She sped away.

Shep took a breath and picked up the first chart and read it.

Then he headed for the number-four bed.

"Dr. Wilde?"

Shep shook himself awake and swung his legs around to get off the bed. "Yes?"

"Dr. Simms is here to relieve you. I'm leaving, too. My husband is here with his four-wheeler, and we can give you a lift home if you'd like." It was Helen, the nurse he'd been working with all night.

Shep checked his watch: 4:12 a.m. At two, the emergency room had been vacant for several hours, and he'd laid down to catch a nap.

"Things have been quiet since midnight," Helen continued in a voice heavy with exhaustion. "Do you want that ride? My husband's waiting for me."

"Sure do. Thanks. I'll grab my things." He hurried to the locker room, put his jacket on over his greens, rolled his other clothing into a bundle and rushed back to where Helen was waiting for him.

Dr. Simms walked up and greeted him. "Good night or bad, Shep?"

"Busy at first, then slow. Is the weather any better out there?"

"Afraid not."

Shep followed Helen out the door, where a huge four-wheel-drive pickup was parked with its engine running. It was still snowing and blowing, and so cold Shep thought his face would freeze before he got into that truck.

When they were seated, Helen said, "Dr. Wilde, this is my husband, Bill."

Shep peered around Helen to see the man at the wheel. "Hello, Bill. Listen, I really appreciate this ride and I hate asking, but would you make one stop before dropping me off? My father is at Myrtle Shank's house, and I'd sure like to check on them and make sure they're okay."

"I know Myrtle. Might even know your dad. Lucas Wilde?"

"Yes, Lucas."

"Don't mind going out of our way at all, Dr. Wilde. Just give me the directions," Bill told him.

Even the four-wheeler had trouble getting through so much snow, Shep noticed. During the drive, he caught sight of the town's two plows, and some of the streets were clear, so the plows were making some headway.

But the wind was a defeating aspect of the storm, rapidly refilling plowed streets with mounds of snow.

Shep gave Bill the directions to Mrs. Shank's house, but a drive that normally took ten minutes went on for a half hour.

"That's Mrs. Shank's house," Shep was finally able to say. Bill stopped the truck, and Shep jumped out and ran—

or tried to run—to the house. He pounded on the front door. "Dad? Mrs. Shank?"

After a minute, Lucas opened the door. "Shep! How'd you get here? Come inside."

"Friends with a massive four-wheeler brought me. They're waiting, so I can't be long. Are you and Mrs. Shank all right?" Shep stayed on the porch and talked to his dad through a crack in the door.

"We're making it, Shep, same as everyone else. Sure am glad I came down here, though. She'd never have been able to weather this on her own."

"You're staying, then."

"Have to, son. I can't leave her alone in this."

"Okay. Oh, by the way, I turned on the faucets in the house."

"Good. I was worried about that. Should've known you'd think of it, but then I really didn't know if you were home or still at the hospital."

"I've been back and forth, via snowmobile mostly. I've got to go, Dad." Shep was shivering. The wind was as sharp as a knife, penetrating his greens and even his heavy jacket. "This can't last much longer, do you think?"

"Hope not, son. Sure hope not."

Shep hurried back to the truck. "It's only about a mile down this same road to Dad's place. That's where I'm staying," he told Bill.

When he was dropped off, however, he slogged through the snow to Andrea's door and knocked. Shuddering from the cold, he tried the knob and was surprised when it turned.

Stepping inside, he closed the door and flipped the lock. The house was black as pitch, and he felt his way through the living room and down the hall to Andrea's bedroom. There was a pocket of fear in his system, for he couldn't imagine her going to bed with the door unlocked. Neither could he visualize her going somewhere and leaving the house open.

Stopping at her bedroom doorway, he peered in, squinting to make the most of what light there was. Was she in that bed, which he could just barely discern?

"Andrea?" he said. Gingerly approaching the bed, he said her name again. There was a small movement under the blankets, but that was all. It was enough to dissolve Shep's qualms, however. She was all right, sleeping soundly, and he probably shouldn't awaken her.

The cold was getting to him, and there was no place to go to warm up. His own bed at his dad's house would warm up after he was in it awhile, but Andrea's bed was already warm.

He didn't think about it very long, because he was starting to shake from the below-zero temperature. Throwing off his clothes with the speed of light, he lifted a corner of the blankets and eased himself into Andrea's bed. Sliding over, he began feeling the warmth of her body. That heat was like a magnet. Without a qualm, he wrapped himself around her and sighed from the pure pleasure of her warmth against his icy skin.

"Wha . . . ?" she said drowsily. "Shep?"

"It's me, honey. I'm cold, and you're toasty warm." He snuggled closer, molding his body to hers. "Oh, that feels good."

She was starting to wake up. "You got in bed with me?"

"You saved my life, honey. I was freezing to death."

She believed him, because the cold of his body was battling the warmth of hers. "What time is it?"

"About five in the morning." He was beginning to think beyond simple warmth. "What've you got on?"

"A sweat suit and socks. How'd you get in?"

"The front door was unlocked."

"Shep, I *never* leave my doors unlocked. You must have picked the lock." Goodness, if he could pick her locks, anyone could. And she'd felt so safe in this house.

"I swear it was open, Andrea. I knocked and called your name, then tried the knob. Your front door was not locked."

"You mean I came to bed last night with the door unlocked?"

"Apparently." He was getting as toasty as her and starting to think of things other than freezing temperatures and warm beds. She felt incredible against him, and he wasn't in just any bed, was he? His hand began moving up and down her back, which, of course, was covered with the fleecy fabric of her sweat suit. "I take it you were warm enough to sleep well," he said.

"Once the bed warmed up last night—early evening, actually—I slept very well." She was very aware of his curious, rather brazen hand exploring her back, but she wasn't above teasing him a little by pretending she was noticing nothing. "Is it still storming? Tell me it isn't. Tell me today is going to be normal in every way. Especially, tell me you heard the electricity is going to be back on at . . . six o'clock."

Shep whispered in her ear, "Wish I could, honey. What I did hear was that so many power lines snapped from the cold and ice, the power company is going nuts trying to get them all repaired. The best news I can give you is that their maintenance crews are working around the clock."

"And it's still snowing," Andrea said with a sigh.

"Afraid so."

Andrea sighed again. "I can't believe my first winter in Montana is a record breaker."

"You're seeing the worst, all right." Shep's voice had gotten a bit husky. He was becoming very aroused from being curled around Andrea. She felt as soft as a plush teddy bear in that sweat suit.

Andrea groaned. "And I have to get up."

"Honey, you'd better stay right where you are. It's awfully cold outside these covers."

"Dr. Wilde, need I explain biology to you, a physician? There are some things one cannot do under these covers."

Catching her drift, Shep chuckled. "Okay, but hurry."

"Don't worry about that," she retorted, sliding out of bed and running from the room to the bathroom next door.

Shep stretched languorously. There were moments in a person's life when he or she felt totally, completely content. This was one of those moments for him. He wasn't only content, he realized, but he was happy. Happy to be in a warm bed during the storm of the century. Happy to be waiting for one special woman to return to his arms.

Andrea made him happy, he thought next. So did his unexciting job, meager wage and being in Rocky Ford again, storm or no storm. What a fool he'd been in California. He had never longed for money and what it could buy until he met Natalie. Then he'd changed. It was as though their meeting had turned him into someone else, into a man who could be molded and shaped by her whims.

Coming home had been the smartest thing he'd done in years. He couldn't remember the precise moment when he'd decided to return to Rocky Ford, and he wished he could because it was a milestone in his life. But it was comforting to know that when things had seemed the darkest, he had made the right move.

Andrea came running in, and Shep held up the covers. Shivering, she jumped into bed. "It must be forty below," she said through chattering teeth.

"Thirty-two below, wind-chill factor seventy below," Shep told her while drawing her into his arms and snuggling her against his warm body.

She snuggled, too. "Oh, you feel good."

"So do you. In fact, you feel so good, I might keep you in this bed for the rest of our lives."

She laughed. "Oh, really?"

"Really. Andrea, I think..." He stopped short of a declaration of love. *Andrea, I think I'm falling in love with you. In fact, I'm pretty certain of it.* But did they really need to talk about love so soon? Couldn't the feeling remain in his system without talking about it? Wouldn't their relationship be stronger without verbal commitments and long discussions about feelings? He would be with her because he wanted to be; she would be with him for the same reason. No promises also meant no criticism because one of them might falter. A relationship with freedom and justice for both of them. What could be better? Certainly not marriage.

Of course, it was a subject he would have to discuss with her. Not now, though. Right now, he wanted to make slow, tender love to her.

"You think what?" Andrea asked.

"Pardon?"

"You started to say something."

"Hmm. Forgot what it was." He grinned and joked. "Must have been a lie."

"No lies, Shep," she said quietly. "Not even in jest." If he lied to her in fun, maybe he would lie about other things, such as one day telling her he loved her when it wasn't true. She could say it right now and mean it, but it would be an awful risk to take.

He raised his head to look into her eyes, and he caught the scent of toothpaste on her breath. "This isn't a lie, okay? I think you're the most beautiful woman I've ever known."

Her breath caught in her throat. "Shep, that can't be true," she whispered.

"Why not?"

Because Lucas said your ex-wife is a stunningly beautiful woman. "Because...because you must know a horde of women."

"That's true, I do. None of them have your looks." Under the blankets, his hand slipped under the top of her sweat suit and cupped her breast. "I'm going to kiss you, beautiful lady," he whispered, slowly bringing down his head.

Andrea closed her eyes just as his lips covered hers. He was going to do much more than kiss her, she knew, and she wasn't going to say no this time. Maybe she would never say no to him again. Maybe she would live out her life just waiting for the times when he came to see her.

Whatever, she loved him madly, and denying herself the physical expression of that love seemed adolescent and silly. So much seemed immature and trivial since the storm had gotten bad. Avoiding that meeting with Charlie, for instance. As soon as the weather permitted an outing, she was going to pay Charlie Fanon a visit. She was going to tell him what she believed, that she was his daughter, and show him her mother's legal documents, Sandra and Charlie's divorce papers and her own birth certificate. She was going to tell Charlie the story Harry Dillon had told her about her birth.

And however Charlie received the information, she would accept it and get on with her life.

"Hmm, sweetheart," Shep whispered against her lips, chasing all thoughts of Charlie and everything else from her mind. "You are dyn-o-mite."

His hand under her top, moving from breast to breast, began working its way downward. "I *could* take this suit off," she said in a throaty, sensuous voice. "Would you like that?"

"I would love it."

Andrea sat up, quickly yanked the top over her head and tossed it to the foot of the bed. Then she slithered back down under the covers and shimmied out of the bottom half of her sweat suit. Shep's skin felt hot against hers.

"You're not cold now," she whispered.

"Honey, I'm one very hot man at the moment."

"I can tell." His naked body wrapped around hers was an arousing sensation, especially the rock-hard evidence of his manhood pressing into her hip.

"That's what you do to me," he told her. "Want to know something? The day we met, Christmas Day...every time I looked at you I thought of sex."

"You didn't! Did you really? I thought you didn't like me. You weren't exactly friendly, you know."

"I wasn't exactly thrilled to be dragged over here, sweetheart. Not only didn't I feel the slightest bit of holiday spirit, I wasn't in a mood to meet anyone. You were a shock, believe me. I thought you'd be about Dad's age, and when you opened the door, I nearly fell over."

"You sure didn't show it," she said dryly.

"Hell no, I didn't show it. I thought you were Dad's girlfriend."

"*What?*" When Shep roared with laughter, she pinched him on the arm. "You devil. You're teasing me."

He nuzzled his mouth into the curve of her throat. "Sorry, but it was too good a chance to pass up. I never thought you were Dad's girlfriend, but I *was* knocked for a loop by your looks. And I did think about sex every time I looked at you."

"Which was why you weren't friendly."

"Probably. It doesn't matter anymore, I'm real friendly now."

Since his hand had crept down to the juncture of her thighs and was doing all sorts of delicious-feeling things to the most sensitive area of her body, she could only gasp, "Yes, aren't you?"

He chuckled deep in his throat. "But you like me friendly, don't you, sweetheart?"

"Yes, I like you friendly," she whispered hoarsely.

He suddenly became very serious. Looking into her eyes, he whispered, "Oh, Andrea, what you do to me."

How could she think of what she was doing to him when what *he* was doing to *her* was so exciting she couldn't lie still? He pushed her legs farther apart and took her mouth in a rough and passionate kiss. That kiss and his caresses between her legs brought her to the brink.

She tore her mouth from his to whimper, "Do it, please do it."

In seconds—using that brief interlude to put on a condom—he was inside of her. Only minutes later, they touched the stars at precisely the same moment.

It was Shep's turn to brave the cold and make a mad dash for the bathroom. Andrea laughed at his haste, then nestled deeply into the blankets.

Had she ever been happier? she asked herself dreamily. Ever, in her entire life?

Love was truly the grandest of emotions.

Ten

Andrea opened her eyes and found herself staring at the ceiling light. It was on!

"Oh, my goodness, the power's back on," she said out loud, gripped by excitement. She sat up and instantly felt the difference in temperature in the house. They must have slept for hours, and at some point during that time, the furnace had started working. "Shep?" she said, grinning broadly, just plain giddy about a shining ceiling fixture and a functioning furnace.

He never budged. She looked at him tenderly for a few moments. Poor dear. He'd had precious little sleep in the past few days, and it would be cruel to wake him just to tell him about the power.

Slipping out of bed, Andrea drew on a robe and slippers, switched off the ceiling light and left the bedroom. There were suddenly a thousand things she could do just because she had electricity.

But first things first. Quickly she went into the kitchen and tried the phone.

"Darn," she mumbled when she heard nothing but silence. But the power was on, and the phone would probably be working very soon, as well.

She stopped to gaze out the kitchen window. The snowflakes that were falling from a gray sky were so minute the air appeared almost misty. Actually, it looked more like frost than snow. Her backyard was one huge sheet of snow, with bumps and mounds indicating shrubs and bushes. It was so deep that it covered most of the fencing between her place and Lucas's, and the trees protruding from it looked black and lifeless, as though their spirit had retreated to a secret place until the weather warmed up.

It looked bitterly cold, and she wished she had a thermometer on a post, as Lucas did in his backyard.

The dripping faucet caught her attention, and she turned the hot-water tap on full blast to check its temperature. The water wasn't hot, but it was warm enough for a shower and shampoo, which seemed to Andrea like the very height of luxury. Anxious to get to that shower, she hastily put on a pot of coffee to brew.

The radio was on, because it had been on when the power failed, and Andrea heard a broadcaster say cheerfully, "It's thirty below zero, folks, so keep those pipes covered and take care when you go outside." Grimacing, Andrea turned down the radio so it wouldn't disturb Shep. Let him sleep for as long as he could, she thought while heading for the bathroom.

She gloried in the simple act of standing under a stream of warm water in the shower stall, and then nearly wept with joy over being able to use her hair dryer and curling iron. The extended storm had definitely altered her outlook on life. And it might not be over yet, she reminded herself. Considering the intense cold, it was possible for the power to go out again.

But she was going to enjoy it while she could. Tiptoeing into her bedroom, she got fresh underwear and a clean sweat suit, then returned to the bathroom to dress. She felt so alive, so good, that she put on makeup and smiled at herself in the mirror. Was it the electricity in the house or being in love that had her eyes sparkling like that? she thought happily.

Yes, she was definitely in love. Every relationship she'd ever had with a man—only a few of them sexual—paled in comparison to her feelings for Shep. And he must care for her in the same lovely way. Who would have dreamed that she would find her soul mate in Rocky Ford, Montana?

Sighing ecstatically, she tidied the bathroom, then deserted it for the kitchen. The coffee was ready, and she poured herself a cup. The refrigerator was running, and it was music to Andrea's ears. Her little rental house was once again cozy and comfortable, and Shep was in her bed. Everything was perfect.

Except for that darned phone. Frowning, she tried it again. Nothing. Questions bombarded her. How was Kathleen faring? Had her other employees been able to get to work and put out Saturday's edition? And how on earth would she, Andrea, ever clear her driveway of so much snow? Even when her street finally got plowed—she could tell it was still snowed in, as there wasn't any traffic—there was still her driveway preventing the use of her car.

But surely she could hire someone to do it. Shep might know people who did that sort of odd job. And if he didn't, Lucas would. She would not worry about that right now.

Noticing her growling stomach, Andrea went for a bowl of cereal. But she stopped midway; a bowl of cereal was not what she wanted for breakfast.

Feeling domestic and lighthearted, she baked some blueberry muffins, broiled bacon until it was crisp and made a pan of scrambled eggs.

She was eating when Shep walked in, looking sleepy-eyed and only half-awake. He had on the green pants from his hospital uniform.

She smiled. "Hi."

"Hi. The power's on."

"Isn't it fabulous? I've already had the most wonderful shower. Are you hungry? I cooked enough for four people."

"I need some of that coffee first. Then I'll wash up and eat." Andrea got up to get him a cup from the cabinet. "Is the phone working, too?" Shep asked.

She shook her head. "I wish it were." She set the cup of steaming coffee on the table. "Sit here and wake up," she said teasingly.

He sent her a smile without any verve or energy behind it.

She put her hands on her hips. "Are you one of those people who are grouchy when they first wake up?"

Shep took a sip of his coffee and cocked an eyebrow at her. "Are you one of those people who aren't?"

"I am this morning." Andrea resumed her place at the table. "I couldn't believe my eyes when I saw the ceiling light burning in the bedroom. Shep, we take so many things for granted." She laughed gaily. "I've been like a kid in a candy store, using my hair dryer, the stove, even listening to the refrigerator running."

"You've been listening to the refrigerator?" Shep said dryly.

"Yes, and don't you dare poke fun at me," she said in a mock-threatening voice.

"Wouldn't dream of it." He was finally waking up, and her appearance was registering. "How come you're so damned beautiful, lady?"

Her cheeks got pink. "I told you I took a shower."

"I'm not talking about clean, sweetheart, I'm talking about beautiful."

Happiness made even her skin glow. "I believe you really mean that."

"Count on it." Rising, Shep walked over to the counter and refilled his cup. "Do you think there's enough hot water for me to shower?"

"It wasn't hot when I showered, but it's probably good and hot now." She couldn't take her eyes off him. Even with whisker stubble on his face and his hair tumbled and awry, he was still the most gorgeous man she'd ever seen. And she loved him madly.

"See you in a few," Shep said, starting from the room. "Oh, you wouldn't have a razor and an extra toothbrush lying around, would you?"

"There's a package of disposable razors in the right drawer of the sink counter, and you can use my toothbrush if you want to." After last night's intimacies, was anything off-limits for them? They hadn't made love only once. It seemed as though every time she had dozed off, she'd been brought out of it by Shep's searching hands and hungry mouth. It had, without a doubt, been the most sensual night of her life.

But it hadn't been night, had it? He hadn't even gotten here until five this morning. Which meant that he had made love to her three times in rapid succession.

What a man, she thought proudly, as though his sexual prowess were her own.

But in a way, it was. Had she ever responded so ardently to any other man?

"I'll keep breakfast hot," she called as he left the room with his cup of coffee. Sighing with a brimming happiness, she got up to put everything in the oven.

Andrea was still sitting at the table when Shep came back. He looked shiny clean, smelled of soap and shampoo and was wearing his own clothes.

"Where on earth did you get those?" she asked, mystified.

"I didn't have time to change at the hospital, so I brought them with me. You just didn't notice the bundle I was carrying."

"Maybe that's because I can't see in the dark." He laughed, and she could tell any grouchiness he'd awakened with had dribbled down the drain with his shower water. "Have a seat," she told him while getting to her feet. "I think you need to be fed."

"I think *you* need to be kissed." Snaking out an arm, he caught her around the waist and looked into her eyes. "Was last night an erotic dream or did it really happen?"

"It happened," she said with her heart in her throat. She lifted a hand to caress his cheek, then stood on tiptoe to press her mouth to his.

He reacted instantly, squeezing her to himself, kissing her with so much heat and passion she thought she would melt. *What's next for us, Shep? Do you love me as I love you?* If only he would say it.

He didn't. With a grin of pure pleasure, he said instead, "Now you can feed me. Food first, fun later."

Andrea's heart sank a little. Was "fun" all this was to him?

No, she couldn't think like that. He'd just come out of a bad divorce and simply wasn't ready for the same kind of commitment she was. Time would take care of that problem. She must be patient.

When the food had been devoured and they were lazily sipping coffee at the table, Shep said, "Now I think it's time we talked about Andrea Dillon."

She nearly choked on her coffee. "Very dull subject," she said with a false laugh.

"Dull?" His eyes twinkled at her above his cup as he took a swallow. "Are you calling last night dull?"

"I'm calling my personal history dull. Shep, please, there isn't anything to talk about." The problem was there was so much she could tell him that she didn't know where to begin. Besides, she didn't want him to know about Charlie just yet. Depending on Charlie's reaction to meeting a daughter he'd either turned his back on before her birth or didn't know he had, she might *never* want Shep to know the story.

Perhaps the only thing she knew for certain at this point was that she wasn't prepared to talk about Charlie Fanon today. And why was Shep so curious today? Because of last night? Because he, too, knew they were in love and felt the normal drive to learn all he could about the woman he loved?

There was some satisfaction in that conjecture, but Andrea still couldn't reveal the secret she had been living with since her mother died. It had become so embedded in her system it felt like a part of her. Exposing it—even to the man she loved—before she talked to Charlie would be like ripping out a vital organ.

She raised her cup to her lips and looked at Shep across the small table. "Why don't we talk about you instead?"

His eyes dropped to his cup. "I'm not sure I can."

He was more honest than she was, Andrea thought uneasily. At least he had admitted a discomfort over the prospect of discussing his past. All she'd done was lie and act as though she had no story to tell.

Abruptly she got to her feet. "Well, what's on the agenda today? Is someone going to pick you up and get you to the hospital for your shift?"

"I don't know what's going on. I think the whole town's confused, Andrea. People are doing what they can and helping each other out in a way we should all be proud of. But schedules are totally defunct, and it's as though the clock stopped when the storm hit."

"Yes, it does feel that way," she murmured as she started clearing the table. "Why don't you build a fire in the fireplace while I tidy the kitchen? I'm also going to chance putting a beef roast in the oven. Say a prayer that the power doesn't go off again. If it does, I'll have a pan of raw meat on my hands."

Shep looked at her queerly. He found it almost impossible to talk about his past, but it wasn't so distant that the sharp edges had worn off. What was Andrea's excuse for eluding such a discussion?

"All right," he said quietly. He'd build the fire and see what happened. Maybe a lazy afternoon together would loosen both of their tongues. It wasn't that he didn't want Andrea to know the facts of his life in California or what he'd gone through over the divorce. It was just hard to get the words out of his mouth.

But there was something in Andrea's past she wouldn't or couldn't talk about, and that was not a new thought. He'd felt it right from their first meeting, along with all of that unexpected sexual tension.

Bending to lay paper and kindling on the grate, Shep continued that line of thought. Andrea was quite a woman. Could any other have lifted him from the doldrums as she had done? He felt something very powerful and potent for her. Maybe it was love. But if it was, there was more than one kind of love between a man and a woman, because it sure didn't resemble the simpering giddiness he'd initially experienced with Natalie.

Andrea made him feel strong, capable and ten feet tall. Natalie had all but castrated him. What in heaven's name had made him think that those ludicrous cravings she had instilled in him had demanded marriage?

As he mulled it over, it was possible to think that he had never really loved Natalie and what he was now feeling for Andrea was the real thing.

But he would never rush into that kind of commitment again. As powerful as his feelings were for Andrea, she would have to take him as he was.

The fire was blazing nicely. He could hear Andrea moving around in the kitchen. He went to the front window, looked out and shook his head. There was more snow on the ground than he could ever remember seeing in Rocky Ford. If they should have a sudden thaw and all that snow turned to water, the whole town would be flooded.

Leaving the window, he drifted absentmindedly around Andrea's small living room. He stopped for a moment to look at the books in her bookcase, then started drifting again. A black notebook on a table caught his eye, and he picked it up and flicked it open.

As he went through the pages, a frown between his eyes got deeper and deeper.

Andrea walked in with a big smile and a plan to make the most of the day. They were warm, comfy, alone and with no way to go anywhere or even talk to anyone on the phone. She had a dinner menu in mind, and the roast was already in the oven. As long as the electricity stayed on, being snowed in with the man she loved could not be considered a hardship.

She noticed his concentration on something in his hands. He was turned a little, so she saw more of his back than his front. But then, as she moved around him, she realized what he was reading. Her outrage was instantaneous and genuine.

Jerking the notebook out of his hands, she said angrily, "Does the word *privacy* mean nothing to you?"

At first, Shep just looked startled, but then his eyes narrowed on her. "Why are you keeping a diary about the Fanon family? When Charlie was mentioned on Christmas, you asked Dad what kind of man Charlie Fanon was. So you don't know him. You don't know *any* of them, so why the chronicle?"

Andrea was clutching the notebook to her chest. "I don't have to explain anything to you."

"No, you don't. You don't have to explain anything to anyone, but that notebook is mighty peculiar, Andrea. What are the Fanons to you?"

Andrea's initial anger was slipping away, being replaced by a weak-kneed dread. She didn't want to have this conversation. Not yet, at any rate. How could she have been so careless as to forget that she'd left the notebook lying on that table?

Still, Shep had had no business in even touching it, let alone reading it.

"I am not going to answer your questions," she told him with a defiant tilt to her chin. "And let me say this. If I were at *your* home, I would never snoop through your things."

"Picking up a book and thumbing through it is snooping to you?"

"You had to know from the first page that this is no ordinary book. Yes, I'd call what you did snooping."

"If you're so touchy about anyone seeing that notebook, why was it in plain sight?"

Her voice rose shrilly. "I forgot it was there, okay?"

"You're mad as hell that I saw it," Shep accused.

"I'm mad as hell that you would *snoop* into my private affairs!"

"Dammit, I wasn't snooping! I wasn't even curious when I picked up that notebook." He paused for a breath. "I'm curious now, Andrea, *extremely* curious. What are you hiding that concerns the Fanons? Why did you clip and keep articles from the newspaper about them? Why have you been watching Charlie's house? Why did you write, 'A man in a dark vehicle spotted my car parked across the street from Charlie's home and tried to follow me tonight. Thank God I lost him. I was so frightened.'?"

She felt as though something were squeezing the breath out of her. "I . . . I can't talk about it."

Shep folded his arms across his chest and looked at her with a militant expression. "Why not?"

"Why can't *you* talk about some things?" she retorted. "I have the same right to privacy as you do, you know. When you said at breakfast that you couldn't talk about your past—meaning your divorce, I'm sure—did I pressure you about it? No, I did not. What I did do, in case you've already forgotten, was to drop the subject. You see, *I* respect *your* right to privacy. Why don't you try giving me the same courtesy?"

Shep unfolded his arms and pointed at the notebook. "Because that thing scares me."

"It *scares* you? That's absurd," she scoffed.

"It's unnatural to keep a diary on a family you don't even know."

"You're a plastic surgeon, not a psychiatrist. Don't try to analyze me and my notebook, Shep. I have a very good reason for keeping up with the Fanons, and it's neither unnatural nor abnormal. You're angry because I won't explain it, which is just too bad because I have no intention of explaining anything about it until I'm ready."

"Meaning that you intend to explain it one day? When, Andrea? What are you waiting for?"

There was sarcasm in his voice, which outraged Andrea all over again. "That is none of your business," she said sharply.

He was silent a moment, then asked, "Are *you* any of my business, Andrea? I've been thinking you are, but maybe I'm wrong. Why don't you set me straight on that point?"

She, too, was silent—painfully so—before speaking. "Are you actually bringing this disagreement down to that? Does it really have anything to do with how we feel about each other?"

"I'm bringing it down to trust, Andrea. Obviously, you have some sort of secret, and just as obviously, you have no intention of sharing it with me. Ergo, you don't trust me. This is different than my not wanting to talk about my past. You're doing something—" again he pointed at the notebook in her arms "—that might even be criminal. At the very least, it's psychologically unsound. And I don't have to be a psychiatrist to see that."

Her voice became ice cold. "Don't you 'ergo' me, Shep Wilde. You might be a doctor, and you might be educated and smart, but your diagnosis of my actions is pure hogwash. I have never committed a criminal act in my life, nor am I 'psychologically unsound.' I think you should leave now. Go and check on your father's house. Maybe some fresh air will clear the ludicrous cobwebs from your self-centered and totally misguided brain."

"You're asking me to leave?"

"I'm *telling* you to leave." She could feel her heart breaking into a million tiny pieces, but he had gone too far.

Shep sucked in a long, slow breath. Then he nodded. "All right, fine. If that's the way you want it, that's the way it will be. I'll get my things."

She watched him walk out of the room and felt as though the sun had suddenly vanished from the universe. Panic seized her. Why not tell him everything? Why not explain the notebook and her reason for keeping it?

Because she couldn't, she thought with a sad sort of finality. She just couldn't. All of her life, she had longed for her father and had grown up thinking he was Harry Dillon. She had made a terrible mistake by not seeing Charlie the day she'd arrived in Rocky Ford, and each day that she'd let slip by with lies and promises to herself of doing it on another day had compounded that error in judgment.

But however painful her procrastination had become, she still couldn't tell anyone—not even the man she loved—about her lonely, fatherless childhood, and about the possibility of finally having a father. It was because she didn't know how Charlie would react to her story, though legally documented. He might want her, or he might not. And if he didn't, if he laughed at her or told her to get lost, she didn't want to be in the position with Shep of having to tell him about it. Which, of course, would be the case if he knew the background of that notebook. If he knew that much, it would only be natural for him to want to know the result of her meeting with Charlie.

No, however much it hurt to see Shep walk out of her life, she could not bare her soul to him.

He returned to the living room wearing his jacket and carrying a bundle of clothing.

"Well," he said with a probing look at her. "I guess this is goodbye."

"It doesn't have to be."

"Doesn't it? Do you think any two people can build a relationship without trust?"

"From where I stand, it appears you're the one without trust. And you're cruel, Shep, very cruel. Accusing me of criminal acts and psychological disorders just because I won't explain my notebook. Do you think I could ever treat you that way? No, it's not me without trust, it's you." Andrea lifted her chin. "So maybe you're right. Maybe this *is* goodbye."

He looked at her for a long time, saying nothing, then strode to the door. He had no more than gone through it when the phone rang.

Miserably unhappy and wiping tears from her eyes, Andrea couldn't even muster up any enthusiasm over the phone working again. Dropping the notebook on the kitchen table, she wiped her eyes again and picked up the phone. "Hello?"

"Duane Kemp, Andrea. Apparently you're still snowed in."

"I haven't seen a sign of a snowplow, Duane. Are you and the others working? I've been feeling very out of touch. The power just came on again this morning, and now the phone, thank God. Maybe things will get back to normal before much longer. I certainly hope so."

"We might have utilities and mobility again, Andrea, but things will never be the same as they were." Duane cleared his throat. "Kathleen . . . Kathleen didn't survive the surgery. I only found out a short time ago. Her housekeeper, Ruth Madison, called. She's been as helpless as the rest of the town as far as communication goes."

Andrea wilted into the nearest chair. "Kathleen's dead?" she whispered. "Oh, no."

Eleven

Andrea wept until her sobs turned to hiccups. Everything was falling apart just when she had started believing in herself. Coming to Rocky Ford had been her first genuine effort to think and act independently, and since, she had been building on that initial independence, slowly and gradually, granted, but making gains nonetheless.

Her mother had been a force to reckon with, and it was not at all comforting to remember just how timidly she had accepted Sandra's demanding ways and almost total lack of interest in Andrea's ideas, opinions and curiosity. For one very good example, why had she permitted her mother to shrug off the questions she had asked about her father?

But Andrea had many questions about her mother's behavior and life-style, questions she would never have answers for. And in the long run, did it matter? Despite Sandra's selfish, self-centered personality, Andrea had loved her and had mourned her death.

However—and this was a real eye-opener—Andrea realized that she did not miss Sandra. Her life had become her own since Sandra's death. Maybe Shep was right, and there *was* something wrong with her emotional wiring.

But Shep had never walked in her shoes, and he couldn't possibly understand what had driven her to devise and maintain that notebook. Even if he knew the whole story, he would never understand why she hadn't immediately confronted Charlie. Perhaps no one would, unless it was someone who had grown up yearning for his or her father, believing he was one man and then finding out that he was a completely unknown name.

Staring out the front window, Andrea sadly wondered if there was any way to resurrect her and Shep's relationship. If only there was a way to go back to that moment when she had walked into the living room and seen him reading her notebook. If there was any such magical opportunity given her, she would handle the situation with tact instead of outrage and anger. It was such an impossible fantasy, she thought with a wounded sigh.

Then there was Kathleen. Andrea moaned out loud, actually feeling physical pain over Kathleen's death.

And the final straw, which she was looking at through the window with her own eyes, was being trapped by a sea of snow. How much longer could she bear being housebound?

But she did have the phone now, didn't she? Turning away from the window, Andrea went to the kitchen and began looking through the Rocky Ford telephone book. Locating the number she'd been thinking of, she dialed it and heard, "Mayor's office. May I help you?"

"I hope so, ma'am. I live on Eastmont Street, and I was wondering if there's some sort of schedule for plowing the town. More to the point, may I expect my street to be plowed anytime in the near future, preferably today?"

The woman sighed. "If you knew how many times I've heard that question in the past few hours... All I can tell you, miss, is that the plows are working around the clock. Eastmont is thinly populated, and while there isn't a strict schedule for clearing the snow for traffic, it's my opinion that Eastmont, and other streets like it, are rather low in priority."

"In other words, you're working outward from the center of town?"

"More or less. Connections to highways were first on the list, and most of the streets in the business areas of town have already been plowed. You do understand the problem, don't you? When it was snowing so hard, they had to repeatedly plow the same arterials."

"What I understand, ma'am, is that I cannot get to my job."

"I sympathize, but everyone living on outlying streets is in the same boat. I myself only got plowed out this morning, and nearly every business that has reopened its doors has employees who cannot get to their jobs."

It was hopeless. This lady was pleasant and kind, but she had no control over the plows. And what good would it do to badger the person or persons who did?

"Thank you for your time," Andrea said, and put down the phone.

She felt an almost hysterical urge to giggle and had to choke back the sensation. For God's sake, what was there to laugh about?

The truth was that the whole thing was getting to her, and she couldn't help it. Shep walking out of her life, Kathleen's death and being snowed in for days and Lord only knew for how much longer were major catastrophes. Who had a better right to hysteria?

She suddenly wanted to know more about Kathleen's demise than Duane had told her. Searching the phone book again, she found Kathleen's home number and dialed it.

"Osterman residence," a female voice said in her ear.

"Is this Ruth Madison?"

"Yes, it is."

"Ruth, this is Andrea Dillon. Do you remember me? I came to see Kathleen—"

"I remember you, Miss Dillon."

"Ruth, I'm in shock over Kathleen, and I know so little about what happened. Can you talk about it?"

"I can tell you what I know, Miss Dillon. About two weeks ago, Kathleen thought she was coming down with the flu. She was always such a live wire, however, and she would not stay home and rest. The next day, she awoke with extreme tightness in her chest. I got worried about pneumonia and insisted she see her doctor. She called me later that day from Missoula. After an examination, the doctor had lined up some very serious tests for her at the clinic, to be done at once. Kathleen tried to make light of her doctor's paranoia, as she called it, but I could tell she was concerned. He had even demanded that she not drive herself to Missoula, and she'd had a friend take her there.

"She was there for three days, then came home with the diagnosis. It was her heart, and I couldn't begin to repeat the medical terms she recited to me. But she needed immediate surgery. In fact, they wanted to keep her there and do the surgery on an emergency basis.

"She refused because, as she told me when she arrived home, she couldn't die and leave so many loose ends. I thought she was kidding, and laughed with her over the silly idea of her dying from a surgical procedure. But, you see, I didn't realize the seriousness of her condition. For days, she dashed around like a madwoman, seeing to the newspaper, visiting her accountant and lawyer and, in general, wearing herself out to tie up those damned loose ends." Ruth's voice broke, but then she continued.

"One of her final tasks was calling you. By then, she could barely get around, which you saw for yourself. She died on the operating table, Miss Dillon. Neither the doctors nor the clinic were at fault. Kathleen's condition came on fast and was deadly serious. If she would have consented to the emergency surgery they wished to perform, there's a very good chance that she would be alive today. I don't know what else I can tell you."

Tears were coursing down Andrea's face, and her voice was thick when she asked, "Her funeral?"

"I'm sick at heart over that, Miss Dillon. Kathleen left strict orders that should she not survive the operation, she was to be cremated at once."

Andrea's eyes widened in shock. "You don't mean it."

"Sad to say, I do mean it. I'll be leaving her house when the weather permits. It's completely snowed in."

"So is mine," Andrea choked out. "Ruth, thank you for talking to me."

"It didn't make you feel any better, though, did it? I'm so angry about it I could spit. Kathleen didn't have to die. Why was that damned newspaper more important to her than her health? So what if there were loose ends dangling all over Montana? Well, there's no point in haranguing you or anyone else about it. It was good of you to call, Miss Dillon. Perhaps we'll meet again."

"Perhaps. Goodbye, Ruth."

Andrea wept for Kathleen again, then found herself crying over the disagreement with Shep. She loved him, and he would probably never speak to her again.

Could any one human being be more miserable than she felt right now?

Shep called Myrtle Shank's house and talked to Lucas. What he really wanted to ask was, *Dad, do you know anything about the notebook Andrea is keeping on Charlie Fanon and his family?* What he said instead was, "How are you and Mrs. Shank?"

Lucas said they were doing okay and then asked about him. "Been able to get to work?"

"In a sporadic fashion," Shep said.

"The weather report is encouraging."

"I haven't had the radio or TV on. What's the prediction?"

"A warming trend. Very little if any snow."

"God, yes, that's encouraging. I think the town is gradually being plowed out. I hope they get to Eastmont soon. I'm about to go stir-crazy. Dad, I could probably get you home if you're ready to come." Shep was thinking of Jerry and his snowmobile.

"When the street is plowed, Shep. I always thought Myrtle had no family, but there's a niece who lives in Tucson, Arizona. Apparently, she's asked Myrtle to spend the winters in Tucson with her, and after the past week Myrtle can't wait to go. Anyway, I'll hang around and keep an eye on her until the street is plowed.''

"All right."

They chatted a while longer, with Shep talking about one thing and thinking another. He couldn't get his mind off that notebook. He'd been in such shock over it that he'd said some harsh words to Andrea, and it was entirely possible that a psychologist or psychiatrist would tell him to mind his business and stay out of Andrea's. She had been right about one thing: he might be a doctor but he was definitely not trained to analyze unusual behavior.

Or what *he* considered unusual. An expert in the field of behavorial disorders might think otherwise.

After goodbyes with Lucas, Shep pondered it all again. He would not rest until he got some advice, he finally had to admit. And the best man he knew to go to for that advice was Dr. Kyle Simmons, an old friend in California.

Shep had to think about calling Kyle for some minutes, as he'd told no one where he was going when he'd left California. His state of mind at the time had demanded a total break with everything and everyone familiar, and there was little question that Kyle would be surprised to hear from him.

But his state of mind had changed drastically, hadn't it? Didn't he feel in control of his life again? Mentally and emotionally strong again?

Yes, yes and yes, he thought, going to his bedroom for his address book. He could talk to Kyle with equanimity, and should Natalie's name come up, he could handle that, as well.

His composed retrospection was a revelation of sorts and made him feel good. In truth, the only concerns he now felt lay with Andrea. He definitely needed some professional advice about that notebook, and Kyle was his man.

Confidently he dialed California and Kyle's office. The normal rigmarole ensued. Dr. Simmons was busy with a patient. Yes, he would receive Dr. Wilde's message to return his call at the first possible moment. Shep gave the receptionist his number and hung up.

The phone rang twenty minutes later. With a cup of coffee in hand, Shep sat down to answer it. "Hello?"

"Shep, you old son of a gun! What in hell are you doing in Montana? You can't imagine the speculation that occurred when you disappeared."

"I can imagine it very well," Shep said dryly. "How are you, Kyle?"

"Busy, rich and handsome as ever," Kyle said with a laugh. "But what's going on with you? How come you're in Montana?"

"It's my home, Kyle. I told you that."

"Hmm, guess you did. So you went home."

"I didn't call to be analyzed via long distance, Kyle, so stop those wheels from spinning in your brain."

Kyle laughed. "Well, whatever your reason for calling, I'm glad to hear from you. Say, I ran into Natalie just last weekend. Saturday night. Party at the Rodale mansion. Everyone who is anyone was there."

Shep recognized boredom in his system. He couldn't care less about Hollywood parties and, in fact, realized that he had *never* enjoyed them. Yet he'd attended hundreds during his marriage and had put on the same phony displays of pleasure that everyone else had.

Shaking his head in self-disgust, he attempted to change the subject. "Listen, Kyle, the reason I called—"

It was as though he hadn't said a word, and Kyle rambled on. "I heard your name at least a dozen times, my friend. Hey, do you remember a guy named Hale Jackson? He was Natalie's date at the party and said he'd been a patient of yours. Had a nose job. Big, good-looking guy. He's an actor and apparently has a good part in Brad's latest picture."

"Don't remember him," Shep said tersely. "Kyle, I need some professional advice. It has nothing to do with me, but I have a friend who—"

"That's what they all say," Kyle broke in with a laugh.

"Dammit, Kyle, would you get serious?"

"Well, aren't we testy?"

"Sorry, but this is important."

Kyle's voice became noticeably cooler. "Fine. I bill for telephone consultations, you know."

"Then bill me, but first answer a few questions. I have a friend who is keeping very close tabs on a family she professes not knowing. She has gone so far as to maintain a detailed diary on their activities, covering a period of about eight, nine months. From what I can gather, she came to Rocky Ford—that's my hometown—last spring and started her diary almost immediately. Now, here's my question. As a professional, would you consider that abnormal behavior?"

"How can you be so sure she doesn't know those people?"

"She said so."

"She could be lying."

"I don't consider her a liar."

"Based on the few facts you've given me, she either knows those people or wants to know them."

"Well, hell, if she wants to know them, all she has to do is walk into the man's place of business. He owns a small coffee shop and he's just about as friendly as anyone can be. That theory doesn't hold water, Kyle."

"Then how about dangerously obsessive? Or maybe she's a stalker."

"She's not deranged, Kyle."

"How do you know? Mental disorders come in many disguises, my friend. Sounds like she could use some behavior therapy. Can you talk her into seeing a psychiatrist?"

Shep heaved a discouraged sigh. He couldn't believe Andrea was mentally unbalanced, but her obsession with the Fanon family could in no way be construed as normal behavior, either. Kyle had told him nothing he hadn't already known. What had he hoped to accomplish with this call, to hear a specialist say that there was nothing abnormal about a person keeping a detailed diary on a family of strangers?

"Well, thanks for talking to me about it," Shep said quietly.

"This woman means something to you, doesn't she?"

"That's neither here nor there, Kyle."

"Just think twice before you get involved with an obsessive woman, my friend. That's probably the best advice I can give you with the little information you've given me."

"Probably is," Shep said, agreeing merely to not disagree.

"When are you coming back to California?"

"I'm not. Goodbye, Kyle. Stay happy." Shep put down the phone.

Andrea received a telephone call that evening. She ran to the phone, praying it was Shep.

She was sadly disappointed. "Miss Dillon, this is Dave Collins. I was Kathleen Osterman's accountant for many years."

Andrea put thoughts of Shep aside for the moment. "It's very nice of you to call, Mr. Collins. Kathleen told me about her arrangement with you."

"Oh, she did? Then my call won't be the surprise I thought it might be. Miss Dillon, I'm going to close the newspaper office."

"I beg your pardon?" She couldn't possibly have heard right.

"I'm closing the newspaper office, stopping the presses, so to speak."

"But you can't do that. Kathleen told me that she had given you explicit instructions to keep the paper operating and put it up for sale."

"What Kathleen did was give me power of attorney to sell the paper, Miss Dillon. Without Kathleen, there is no newspaper. Let me put it another way. Right now, the *Rocky Ford News* is worth a great deal of money. It won't be if I permit inept employees to run it into the ground."

"Kathleen's employees are not inept!"

"I think I know a little more about it than you do, Miss Dillon. If I understand correctly, you worked for the paper one day. That hardly makes you an expert."

"I would have been on the job if not for the storm. Mr. Collins, please reconsider. Duane Kemp and the others need their jobs. And they are not inept. They're very capable people, and—"

"They are drones, Miss Dillon, nice people, granted, but employees who merely did as they were told by a very strong-willed and intelligent woman. Kathleen was the backbone of that company, and nothing survives without a backbone."

A sob welled in Andrea's throat. Her voice became husky. "This is not what Kathleen wanted, and you know it. How can you do this with a clear conscience?"

"I'll worry about my conscience, Miss Dillon. You will receive a check for your day of work. Good night."

"Rocky Ford will be without a newspaper!" Andrea shouted angrily.

But the line was dead. Dave Collins, a man whom Kathleen had apparently trusted implicitly, had hung up.

Twelve

A rumbling noise awakened Andrea in the middle of the night. Jumping out of bed, she raced through the house to the living-room window. The plows! Oh, thank God, she thought.

She watched until they were out of sight, then returned to bed. Thank God, she thought again while closing her eyes. Things were finally getting back to normal.

Her lids raised as memory and sorrow struck without mercy.

It was hours before she fell asleep again.

Things did get more normal. Andrea was still eating breakfast when a strange man knocked on her front door. Peering through the living-room window before opening the door, she spotted a truck with a plow parked in the street. It wasn't city equipment and appeared to her eyes as the sort of truck ranchers used.

At any rate, she was elated to open the door. She even mustered a smile, no simple feat this morning.

"Morning, ma'am," the man said. His pants were pocked with snow from wading from the street to her door. "I'm plowing driveways. Do yours for fifty dollars."

"Deal," she said without a second's hesitation. If she didn't get out of this house soon, she was going to lose her mind. Besides, she had things to do that required the use of her car.

"And my son will shovel a path from the driveway to your front door for ten dollars," the man said.

"Sounds like you're an enterprising family. Tell your son that he, too, has a deal." She would have paid double the sixty dollars for mobility.

"We'll collect when the jobs are done." Touching the brim of his hat with his gloved fingertips, the man headed for his truck.

Andrea quickly closed the door. During the few minutes it had been open, she had gotten chilled. It might not be snowing, but it was still bitterly cold.

Going to the kitchen for her cup of coffee, she returned to the living room to watch the man and his son efficiently clearing her paths to freedom.

There were unusual energies and emotions flowing throughout Andrea's body this morning. Dave Collins's overbearing, self-serving decision to close the newspaper was one reason; the other was Shep's overbearing, self-serving decision that she must be loony to keep a written record on the Fanon family. Shep's attitude hurt the most, but Dave's was infuriating.

She was not through with either man. If nothing else, each of them was going to get an earful.

And there was one more chore that could no longer be put off. She was going to see Charlie Fanon. Whatever happened, whatever price she might have to pay for bringing such news to a virtual stranger, she was finally determined to do it.

When the man and his son were done with their work, she gladly paid them and then took a moment to relish their achievement. Her driveway was clear, and there was a nice wide path connecting it with her front stoop.

Then she went to her bedroom to change clothes. After fixing her hair and makeup, she put on her heavy overcoat, gloves and scarf, tucked an envelope into her purse, slung it over her shoulder and went to the garage, where she pushed the button to raise the door. She did have a moment of anxiety before turning the key in the ignition of her car; it had been very cold for a very long time, and maybe it wouldn't start.

But the engine only coughed a little before settling into a steady, satisfying hum. Greatly relieved, Andrea let it run for several minutes to warm up. When the heater started working, she put the car in reverse and slowly backed to the street.

What a wonderful feeling it was to be driving again, to be out and about. Apparently, many other people felt the same, as traffic seemed heavier than usual. Passing the town's one supermarket, Andrea noted the crowded parking lot. She would make a stop there today, as well, but later, on her way home.

Her first destination was the newspaper office. With a mountain of snow on each side of every street in town, finding a place to park was not a simple matter. But she finally located a spot not too far from the news office, got out and hiked the distance.

The Closed sign on the inside of the glass door had her gritting her teeth, and the door was locked, as well. But she had a feeling someone would be there, and she pounded on the heavy glass and yelled, "Duane? Sally? Grace? Is anyone in there?"

Duane came walking out of the pressroom. Andrea watched him come to the door and unlock it. "Hello, Duane. Could we talk for a minute?"

"Yes. Come in," he said somberly.

Andrea followed him in and instantly felt like bawling.

But she was done with weeping and ineffective lamentations. This was *her* life, dammit, and it was time she led it instead of meekly permitting it to lead her.

"I was just cleaning out my things." Duane leaned against the counter with a sigh. "What do you want to talk about?"

"Aren't you upset about Dave Collins closing the newspaper?"

"What good would that do? Kathleen gave him power of attorney to do what he wanted with the place."

"That's not true. Kathleen told me in very plain language that she had explicitly instructed Dave to keep the paper open and put it up for sale."

Duane frowned at her. "Why didn't she tell the rest of us that?"

"I have no idea. For that matter, I have no idea why she hired me when she did. But I do know that she did not want the paper shut down. And she trusted Dave to follow her instructions."

"Do you think they're in writing?"

"Is there any way we can find out?"

"Court order?" Duane said speculatively. "But we'd have to hire a lawyer, and I'll tell you right up front that I don't have the money to pay a lawyer, Andrea. And I doubt that Sally or Grace does, either. Especially now, when we're going to have to live without paychecks until we can find other jobs."

I have the money, Andrea thought. But maybe there was a way around hiring an attorney. "Let me ask you something, Duane. Could the four of us, you, Sally, Grace and me, put out a good newspaper?"

Duane gnawed his bottom lip a moment. "If you did what Kathleen did and the rest of us took care of our usual jobs, I don't see why not."

Andrea's heart sank. She was no Kathleen Osterman.

But she was sure willing to give it a shot.

"Okay," she said, conveying a confidence she was far from feeling. "I'm going to pay Mr. Collins a visit. Is your home number in the phone book?" Duane nodded. "I'll be calling you later today. Maybe I'll have good news, maybe not, but I'm not giving up on this without a fight, Duane."

Andrea walked to the door. "Talk to you later."

She had looked up and memorized Dave Collins's office address, and it took only a few minutes to drive there. She walked through his front door with her head held high. There was a woman seated at a desk in a small room with several closed doors in two walls. "I'd like to see Dave, please," Andrea said calmly, deliberately implying that she was on a first-name basis with the accountant. "Is he in?"

The woman smiled. "Yes, he is. May I tell him your name?"

"Certainly. It's Andrea Dillon. Tell him it's very urgent that I speak to him."

The woman picked up the phone and pushed a button. "Mr. Collins, there's an Andrea Dillon in reception who has urgent business to discuss with you. May I send her in?"

Andrea watched the woman's face change from normal to red. "Uh...yes, I'll take care of it," she stammered into the phone. Her gaze rose to Andrea's. "I'm sorry, Ms. Dillon, but he's swamped right now and can't see you."

"That's not what he told you at all, is it?" Andrea smiled sweetly. "What he really said was that he didn't want to talk to me." She glanced at the closed doors; Collins was behind one of them. With another sweet and ladylike smile at the receptionist, Andrea walked around the woman's desk and headed for the nearest door.

"Ms. Dillon, please!" the woman gasped.

Ignoring her plea, Andrea turned the knob and peered into an office. "Sorry," she said to a startled-looking young woman. The second door produced results. A heavyset man glowered at her from behind a massive desk. "Mr. Collins, I presume?" she said, entering and shutting the door behind her.

"Young woman, I could have you arrested for this," Collins blustered.

Andrea calmly sat down. "But you won't, will you? Dave, I'd like to see the paperwork Kathleen gave you regarding her wishes for the newspaper."

"Don't be absurd. Kathleen's and my arrangement is none of your business."

"Perhaps it's the business of the court." Collins's eyes shifted from hers. "Do you think a judge would be interested in your handling of Kathleen's estate, Dave?" Andrea asked in a deliberately innocent voice.

Her tone changed abruptly, becoming hard and determined. "Know what I think, Dave, old pal? I think *you* think that no one has the money to fight your decision to close the paper. Well, think again. You're right about Duane and the other employees, but you're very wrong about me. You see, I have lots of money, and I would just love spending some of it in besting a scoundrel like you in a very public court battle. Oh, yes, I would make sure it was front-page news in every paper in Montana, Dave. Money does have a way of getting things done, wouldn't you agree?"

"You only worked for the paper one damned day. What makes you so high-and-mighty?" Collins snarled.

Andrea leaned forward in sudden anger. "I happen to respect Kathleen's final wishes, you jerk! She trusted you, and you let her down. What in hell kind of professional are you? What kind of man? Either you let me see Kathleen's papers or you reopen the newspaper today. I want Duane Kemp and the others put back to work immediately, or so help me I'll hire the best lawyer that money can buy and run you out of town!"

"You're going to diminish her estate," Collins accused.

"So damned what? You're not the beneficiary, so what's it to you?" Andrea's eyes narrowed. "Wait a minute. What *is* it to you? In terms of dollars and cents, what are you going to get out of Kathleen's estate?"

"That, too, is none of your business."

But Andrea knew she had hit the nail on the head. He was going to receive a percentage of the value of Kathleen's estate, once the paper was sold! Of course. She should have thought of that before now.

Dave Collins was no longer blustering. In fact, he was sweating, and it wasn't from the temperature of the room. Andrea was still wearing her overcoat and was not a bit too warm. Except for being a little hot under the collar.

She got to her feet. "I see it all now, and you know I do. I think it's best if you're the person who calls Duane, Sally and Grace and tells them to return to work in the morning. I'll be there also, and those doors had better be open and that press had better be running." She started for the door.

"The paper's for sale, you know," Collins shouted angrily. "None of you will have your jobs for long. Believe me, you'll get no recommendations from me to the new owner."

Andrea stopped and turned. "Keep your recommendations in one of your desk drawers or shove them up your nose, whichever you prefer, Dave. When the paper is sold, I and the other employees will deal with it. But it had all better be handled as Kathleen wanted, not in a way that will feather your own nest. Goodbye."

On her way out, Andrea sent the worried receptionist another sweet smile. "Dave is just a peach, isn't he?" she said to the harried woman.

Outside, she chuckled all the way to her car. Never had she accomplished so much in such a brazen way. Guts, brains and money were a dynamite combination.

It was especially gratifying to finally realize that she possessed the first two attributes along with her inherited money.

Calling on Charlie Fanon was Andrea's next planned task. She couldn't let the bravado with which she'd dealt with Dave Collins slip away, she told herself while driving to Foxworth Street. In truth, she could not have been in a better frame of mind for finally facing Charlie.

Still, as she drew nearer to Charlie's home, butterflies began developing in her stomach. "No," she said out loud, commanding her system to calm down. She was not going to drive on past Charlie's house, not this time. She was not going to speak to him as she had to Dave Collins, of course, but neither was she going to act like a wimp. If he threw her out on her ear, so be it. But never again was she going to put in a sleepless night worrying about how Charlie Fanon would take her showing up out of the blue with her mother's documents in hand. By tonight, she would know.

There was absolutely no place to park on Foxworth. It was a narrow street to begin with, which Andrea had already known, and the immense banks of snow from the plows completely eliminated any street parking.

But Charlie's large driveway had been plowed or shoveled clean, and there was only one vehicle parked in it, a white pickup that Andrea knew belonged to Charlie.

Boldly she drove into the driveway and parked behind the pickup. But then, after turning off the ignition, she had to take several deep breaths before getting out. Her heart was pounding, and she couldn't help it. For months, she had thought of and suffered over this moment. In all honesty, until meeting Shep and then Kathleen, this moment was practically the only thing that she *had* thought about.

"Well, get to it," she mumbled, forcing her hand to go to the door handle. She climbed out and closed the door quietly, as though a slam would damage the neighborhood ecology in some mysterious way.

Once on her feet, she bravely marched to the street, skirted a huge bank of snow and strode up Charlie's front walk.

Lucas was finally home and darned glad to be there. He told Shep that he was also glad about Mrs. Shank's decision to spend the rest of the winter with her niece in Tucson. "Lady her age should be with family, even in good weather," was Lucas's opinion.

Shep made some lunch while his dad took a shower and got into clean clothes.

Then they sat down to eat and catch up. "Been able to get to work at the hospital?" Lucas asked.

"Off and on." Shep told him again about Jerry's snowmobile and the rides he'd caught with owners of four-wheelers. "Even so, one of them got stuck one night. The snow was up to the truck bed and still coming down. It's a wonder anything moved that night."

"Sure is," Lucas agreed. "It was about as bad a storm as these old eyes have seen." Lucas took a swallow of coffee. "Seen anything of Andrea? I've been wondering how she weathered the storm."

That was the opening Shep had been waiting for. "Dad, to your knowledge, does she know the Fanons?"

Lucas frowned. "Where'd that question come from?"

"Something very odd happened. It's had me going in circles ever since."

"Well, spit it out, boy. What happened?"

Shep set his half-eaten sandwich on his plate. "I spent quite a lot of time with Andrea during the worst of the storm, and—"

"You did?" Lucas grinned. "Don't blame you a bit. She's one very special little lady."

"Yes, she is," Shep said quietly. It occurred to him suddenly that he couldn't discuss that notebook with Lucas, not with anyone in Rocky Ford, for that matter, but especially not with his father. And Andrea *was* special. She was so special that he was in love with her. The forever kind of love. The kind of love he'd never before experienced.

He sat back, stunned by that unexpected revelation.

"Well, what happened that was so odd?" Lucas asked.

"Uh . . . she mentioned the Fanons, and I was under the impression she didn't know them."

"What's so odd about that? Maybe she does know them, or some of them, leastwise."

"It's possible," Shep mumbled, wishing to heaven that he hadn't started this conversation. "Guess it was nothing, after all." He took a big bite of his sandwich, thinking anxiously while he chewed that he had to see Andrea and apologize. And right away, the sooner the better. The minute he and Lucas were through with lunch, in fact. He would go this very minute if it wouldn't prompt a barrage of questions from his dad that he preferred not answering.

Maybe Andrea would not accept his apology. Maybe she was so angry with him she would never speak to him again.

She had a right. How had he had the gall to question her about that notebook the way he'd done, and then make matters worse by suggesting there was something abnormal about a person who kept a diary on a family they didn't know? In the first damned place, what did he know of her friends?

Of course, she could have done just a little explaining.

But there were some things people couldn't talk about. A clam like him was a perfect example. Who was he to decide what Andrea could or could not reveal about herself?

Still . . .

No *stills*, no *buts*. He loved her and if she loved him, what more was there? In fact, he had a darned good argument in favor of a permanent relationship all lined up in his head. *You accept me with my idiosyncrasies, and I'll accept yours, no questions asked. What do you say?*

That was what he had to find out, what Andrea would say the next time they were together.

He couldn't wait a minute longer. Pushing back his chair, he told Lucas, "There's something I have to see Andrea about. See you later."

Lucas merely sat there and chuckled as Shep raced away for a jacket and then out the front door. His son was a fine man, and Andrea was a fine woman. In his opinion, they would make a fine pair.

Shep zipped his jacket as he walked down his dad's driveway to the street. It was great to have the freedom to drive his car again, but it was ironic that the first night he would be able to get to the hospital on his own since the storm had struck was also a night off.

Ironic but great, he added with a hopeful little grin. How he would love curling up with Andrea in front of her fireplace tonight.

Maybe she would love it, too.

Jauntily skipping up the steps to her front stoop, he knocked on her door. After a minute, he knocked again. "Andrea?" he called.

Darn it, she must have gone somewhere. And then, just like that, he knew where she'd gone—to the newspaper office, of course. She had just started her job when the storm immobilized the town. It was only natural for her to hurry down there the minute it was possible to do so.

He headed back to his father's house. He would keep watch and return when Andrea got home.

Andrea opened the door of Charlie's Place, the name he'd given his coffee shop, and heard the tinkling of a small bell. Looking up, she saw it, and for some strange reason, that little bell made her feel less tense.

"Hello, there."

There was only one person in the shop, and he was Charlie Fanon, standing behind the counter and wearing the friendliest smile Andrea had ever seen.

"Hello," she said almost shyly.

"Come on in," Charlie invited. "Don't see too many young folks in here."

Andrea looked around at the empty tables and counter stools. Charlie laughed. "The morning rush hour is over, miss. Besides, I haven't had much business since the storm hit. First, people couldn't get out at all, and now there's no place to park their cars. If they don't live within walking distance, they don't come. Sit anywhere. Can I get you a cup of coffee? Guaranteed to be the best in town."

"It smells very good in here."

"Grind my own beans, ma'am. That's what you're smelling. Nothing better than the aroma of rich coffee beans."

Andrea smiled weakly and perched on a counter stool. Charlie filled a cup with coffee and placed it in front of her. "Cream or sugar? Real cream, ma'am, not that fake stuff."

"I . . . I use milk at home."

"I have milk, if you prefer it over cream." Charlie reached down into his small refrigerator and brought out a carton of milk. "I'll put some in a pitcher," he told her.

She kept sending him quick glances, trying to analyze his features in brief spurts. He'd probably been a very handsome man in his youth, as he was still nice looking. But she could see no resemblance between her own features and his.

Why would she, though? Everyone had always said she was the picture of her mother.

"I've seen you before," Charlie said, setting the pitcher of milk near her cup. "Let's see, where was it? Oh, I remember. You were at Serena's wedding."

Andrea stirred her coffee, then took a sip. "Delicious," she murmured.

"Told you so. Anyhow, am I remembering right? Were you at my daughter's wedding?"

"Yes," Andrea said softly. "And I was also at your niece's wedding, and one day I followed you to church and sat in the back so you wouldn't see me."

Charlie became very still. "You did all that? What's your name?"

"Andrea Dillon."

"I'm Charlie Fanon."

"I know."

"You do? And you know Serena?"

"No. Nor am I acquainted with Lola or Candace or any of their husbands. But I know who they all are."

Charlie shook his head. "You're perplexing me, Ms. Dillon."

"I'm sorry. This...this is very difficult." She was indeed fortunate to have come in when Charlie had no customers. Of course, she could have managed to let him know that she needed to talk to him alone. But as difficult as being here was, it could have been worse.

Charlie's eyes narrowed slightly. "What's difficult, Ms. Dillon?" In the next breath, a shadow of fear clouded his face. "You say you know who each member of my family is. Did something happen to one of them?"

"No, no!" Andrea took a breath. "Please, I never meant to alarm you."

Charlie sank onto a stool behind the counter. "What have you come here to tell me?"

"You *know* I have something to tell you, don't you?"

"Yes. What is it?"

Andrea's hands shook as she opened her bag and pulled out a large envelope. "I'll try to keep it simple," she said, realizing that her voice was trembling as much as her hands. "You were once married to Sandra Keller." "Keller" had been Sandra's maiden name.

"Yes?" Charlie said cautiously, making a question out of the word.

"She...she's my mother. Or she was until last February. She...died then." Andrea's voice had become so weak she could barely hear herself. She cleared her throat. "I...I have reason to believe you're my father."

Charlie was about to say something, but she cut him off and kept talking. Now that she'd gone this far, she wanted the rest over and done with. "You see, she was pregnant when she divorced you. I don't believe she knew it, and when she learned of her condition, she married a man named Harry Dillon. His name is on my birth certificate, but...the dates don't jibe. Anyway, after Mother's death, I located Mr. Dillon and he told me that Mother was pregnant when they married. He agreed to accepting paternal responsibility because he loved her so much.

"And...and then she left Mr. Dillon before I was a year old, and I never got to know him," Andrea said sadly. "He's a very nice man. At least, he was nice when I went to see him last February." Charlie's shell-shocked expression sank in, and she dug into the envelope. "This is a copy of your divorce papers, and this one is my birth certificate."

Charlie picked up the papers and scanned them. After a few moments, his eyes lifted to study her face. "You look like her."

"I know."

"Are you really my daughter?"

"I...think so," she whispered.

Tears suddenly filled Charlie's eyes. "And I never knew about you. How could Sandra have been so cruel? She could have let me know."

"Did she ever contact you about anything after the divorce?"

"Not even to find out if her children were well."

Andrea gasped. "Serena and Ron? Oh, I had hoped so much they were my brother and sister, but..." She stopped to watch Charlie, who had covered his eyes with his hand and appeared to be weeping.

Was he crying out of joy? Regret? Misery? Oh, damn, she thought, finally letting her own emotions go where they may. Tears dribbled down her cheeks, and she blew her nose on a tissue she yanked from her purse.

Charlie reached for a napkin and dried his eyes. "There's more to this story than you know," he said sadly. "When your mother left me in California, she demanded a clean break. She wanted no more of me or of her two babies. She just walked out and got a Nevada divorce. I never heard where she was or what she was doing. I kept thinking she would have a change of heart and want to see her children. It never happened, and after a while I packed up and moved the kids and our belongings to Rocky Ford.

"When Ron and Serena got old enough to ask questions about their mother, I couldn't tell them that she just didn't want them. What child could handle knowing his own mother wanted nothing to do with him?" Charlie sighed. "Anyhow, I lied to them. I lied to my little son and daughter and told them their mother died before they could remember."

"I grew up thinking my father didn't want me," Andrea said, then put her hands over her face. Sobbing, she was not aware of Charlie getting off his stool and walking around the counter.

But then she felt his hands on her shoulders. He turned her stool and put his arms around her. "Your father would have wanted you if he'd known about you," he said softly.

Andrea really lost it then. She sobbed into his shirt and let him pat her back and say, "There, there. Don't cry, child. Everything will be fine, you'll see."

"I...was afraid to come here," she said in a voice almost incoherent from so much hard weeping.

"Why would you be afraid to meet your father?"

"I shouldn't have been. I don't know. At first, I wondered about Lola, and if you'd married again and had another family. And then I read about Ron's tragic death in the paper. The whole family was listed in that obituary article, and I learned about Serena." Another spate of sobs shook her. "Mother robbed me of ever knowing my brother."

"Was she good to you, Andrea?"

"I . . . I can't answer that now. I need to think about it. How could anyone with even a spark of goodness do the things she did?"

"Well, at least she didn't give you up when she learned she was pregnant with you," Charlie said. "See? She did have some good points."

Andrea pushed away from him so she could see his face. "How can you be kind after what she did to you?" Charlie merely smiled, albeit wanly. "What are you going to tell Serena about me?" Andrea asked.

"The truth."

"Then you'll also have to tell her you lied about her mother dying when she was a baby."

"I know."

"Charlie, I didn't come here to cause you any pain."

"You had every right to come here. I'm very happy you came, honey." Charlie smoothed the damp tendrils of auburn hair back from her forehead. "Do you think you can call me Dad?"

Andrea crumpled again. "Yes, oh yes . . . Dad."

Thirteen

Hours later, Andrea arrived home in such a state of euphoria that she turned into her own driveway with absolutely no memory of the drive from her father's house to her own.

Her father. Her *father!* And he was wonderful and kind and loving and positively thrilled to have a second daughter. What a fool she'd been to fear confronting him. She could have been part of the Fanon family from her first day in Rocky Ford.

They had talked nonstop most of the afternoon. Charlie had shown her photograph albums crammed with family pictures and had told her all about Serena's and Ron's childhood and teenage years. Then he'd related Lola's story. In turn, Andrea had told him everything about herself that she thought would interest him.

When she had finally said she should go, he had hugged her with a sentimental tear in his eye and said, "Give me a day or so to talk to the family, especially to Serena. I'm sure everyone will want to meet you right away, so expect to hear from me very soon." Andrea gave him her phone number, her address and a kiss on the cheek.

"I can't imagine why I was so afraid to meet you," she'd said emotionally.

"Given your background, I can imagine why very easily," Charlie had answered. It was the harshest comment he'd made all day in reference to his children's mother, and it was only mildly so. Andrea had never met a nicer, kinder person in her life, and he was her father.

Small wonder her head was spinning as she pulled into her garage. But how she'd made it home on ice and snow without an accident, she would never know, because her mind certainly had not been on the road.

She started into her house with a song in her heart and heard the telephone ringing. Hastening her steps, she dropped her purse on the kitchen table and picked up the phone. "Hello?"

"Andrea, what in heck did you say to Dave Collins?"

She laughed gaily. "Hi, Duane. He called you, right?"

"Called Sally and Grace, too. We're utterly amazed. What'd you do to the guy, hang him by his thumbs or something?"

"I merely told him what I knew to be fact and what I would do about it if he didn't comply with Kathleen's wishes to the letter. You see, what he was counting on was no one putting up a squawk because it could be an expensive undertaking, and I... Oh, just a second, Duane, someone's at my door. Hold on." Andrea laid down the phone and hurried to the front door. "Who's there?"

"Shep."

Her pulse rate was immediately faster. Unlocking the door, she pulled it open and then nearly melted at the sight of him. But she managed to speak normally. "Hi. I'm on the phone. Come in and close the door."

She dashed back to the kitchen. "Sorry, Duane. Where were we?"

"Doesn't matter. We can talk tomorrow. You'll be coming to work in the morning, I expect?"

"Wild horses couldn't keep me away. See you then. Oh, Duane, before we hang up, I'd like your input on something."

"Anything, Andrea. What is it?"

"Well, the four of us are going to be working without a boss, and what I'd like to do is have a meeting in the morning to discuss it. Do you think the women will agree?"

"I don't see why they wouldn't, but Kathleen assigned you her office, didn't she?"

"Yes, and it's too bad that she couldn't have assigned her expertise as easily. I'm no Kathleen, Duane. I don't have the experience or knowledge to take her place. Anyhow, I'm sure if the four of us cooperate, we can turn out a decent newspaper. We do need to talk about it, though."

"Fine with me. I'm sure Sally and Grace will be pleased to participate."

Even though Shep had remained in the living room, he couldn't help hearing Andrea's conversation with a man named Duane, obviously someone who worked at the newspaper office. Although their discussion was mundane enough, it puzzled Shep, because why hadn't it taken place at the news office?

Maybe Duane hadn't been there.

Or maybe it wasn't where Andrea had been all day.

Damn, she was a perplexing woman!

All right, cool it, he told himself firmly. *You're not here to grill or doubt her. She can keep her notebook a secret for the rest of her life, and she can come and go as she pleases without explaining every move to you.* Wasn't that the conclusion he'd come to this very morning? He wouldn't ask questions; she wouldn't ask questions. They would just love each other and be happy.

But it didn't work that way, did it? Frowning, Shep walked to the window and stared out. He loved Andrea and he couldn't stop himself from wanting to know all there was to know about her. He hadn't been that way with Natalie, he recalled. She'd come and gone, and he had rarely asked for a reason. Yes, he'd tried to save their marriage, but he had never liked failure in any form.

His mouth was suddenly dry with dread. Failing with Andrea would be a thousand times worse than his divorce. But failure itself had been his primary nightmare in that dismal case. This time, he would be losing the only woman he had ever *really* loved.

What should he do? What should he say to Andrea?

Tell her you love her, you moron.

Yes, that was the answer. *Bare your soul. Talk about commitment. Hell, tell her you're already committed to her.*

His heart was beating like a tom-tom when she walked into the room. Turning from the window, he watched her hang her coat in the closet.

"Would you like me to hang up your jacket?" she asked.

Good sign, he thought. *She isn't immediately going to throw you out.*

"Yes, thanks." Shedding his jacket, he walked over and handed it to her. There was a smile on her beautiful lips, and a glow in her eyes he'd never seen before. She looked . . . happy.

His heart sank. Something had made her very happy today, and it wasn't him.

"Sit down," she said, moving farther into the living room. Her hand suddenly rose to her cheek. "Oh, good grief. I meant to stop at the supermarket and forgot. I'm out of so many things, but I can offer you a cup of coffee or tea."

"Nothing, Andrea, thanks." His gaze washed over her. "You look beautiful . . . and happy."

Her smile got bigger, brighter. "I am happy. First of all, just getting out of the house was wonderful, and then—"

He took the few steps that separated them and, putting his hands on her shoulders, looked deeply into her eyes. "May I say something?"

Startled by his abrupt interruption, and the fact that his face was mere inches from hers, she blinked. "Uh . . . yes, of course."

She realized that he was nervous, and she'd never seen him nervous before. Brooding, passionate, overbearing and exceedingly desirable, but never nervous.

"Okay, here goes," he mumbled, and took a long breath. "I love you."

She stared blankly. "You what?"

"I love you."

She kept staring, and he kept staring, and finally he said, "Don't you have anything to say to that?"

"Uh . . . yes. What about trust? You talked about trust being so important, and—"

"Love supersedes trust."

"Meaning that you love me but you still think I'm a little off my rocker."

"Absolutely not."

"You said that much too fast, Shep. Are you asking me to believe you're no longer curious or upset about my Fanon notebook?" She was prepared to tell him her entire history, but this trust business was his doing and they had better get it straightened out before talking about love. But, oh, she did love him. So much that she wanted to stop talking altogether and kiss him senseless.

"I'm curious, yes, but I promise to never mention it again. I'm trying to be completely honest with you, Andrea. I've been miserable without you. I can't sleep, can barely eat and the only thing I think of is you. I say to hell with everything but what we feel for each other. What do you say?"

She inhaled sharply. "That was quite a speech."

"It boils down to one thing. Do *you* love *me?*"

"If I said yes, what would you say next?"

"Do it and find out."

"A challenge," she murmured. Her tongue flicked to moisten her lips, and she saw Shep watching the innocuous gesture with a sensual gleam in his eyes.

Well, it was what she felt, too . . . sensual, ecstatic with every event of the day and so thrilled with his declaration of loving her that she felt as though she could fly around the room.

But she knew he still didn't trust her. He thought because she kept a diary on a family of strangers, there had to be something wrong with her mentally. Before anything else occurred between them, he had to learn the truth.

"I want you to hear about my notebook first. I'm willing to talk about it now."

"I only want to hear three words from you right now," Shep growled. "Can you say them?" he demanded.

Why wasn't he getting the message. She tried teasing him out of his mood by laughing lightly. "You're getting awfully serious."

"Dammit, I *am* serious!"

"And now you're getting angry."

Frustrated, Shep let go of her and walked away. He stopped at the fireplace, put one hand on the mantel and looked down at the cold ashes on the grate. "You're not taking me seriously. Will you ever?"

"Shep," she said gently. "I'm sorry. I can say those three words, just as easily as you did, but what do they really mean? *I* think for you they mean that you'd like to take me to bed again." *Say you'll listen to an explanation of my notebook. Say something about a future together. Say you want me in your life for the rest of our days.*

He turned his head to look at her. "Do you expect me to deny a desire to make love to you again? I'd like to rip your clothes off this second. But that's sex, not love."

Her point exactly, although he didn't seem to grasp its subtlety. Damned stubborn man. Fine, she'd play his silly game. But she was going to prove his definition of love in the process. Letting her eyelids droop seductively, she raised her chin and smiled. "If you want to rip off my clothes, why aren't you doing it?"

"Because I want *more!*" he shouted. "Don't you get it?"

"Oh, dear, now you're really angry. Let's see if we can't cheer you up." Slowly Andrea began unbuttoning her blouse. Sliding it from her arms and shoulders, she dropped it on the carpet. The look on Shep's face was one to cherish. Laughing deep in her throat, she kicked off her boots and stepped out of her slacks. They, too, ended up on the carpet.

Then, clad in a lacy rust-colored bra and matching panties, she slithered in blatantly female fashion toward the hall. "That was merely a preview of the main event," she said in her most provocative voice. "Which will take place in my bedroom, if you're interested. Tootle-oo, darling."

Shep stared after her, as stunned as if he'd been struck by lightning. Then he raced from the room and stopped at her bedroom door, which was hanging open. She had already removed her bra and was sliding her panties down her legs.

"What took you so long?" she said with the sexiest expression he'd ever seen on any woman's face. Throwing back the blankets, she got on the bed and stretched. "Hmm, feels good." Her expression became one of a temptress. "But you can make me feel much better, can't you, darling?"

"Andrea..." He heard the helpless note in his voice and didn't like it. Okay, so she'd taken him by surprise. But if she wanted to play like this instead of talking about love, so be it. He walked close to the bed and began undressing.

She watched every move he made, and when he was naked she raised his blood pressure by staring at his manhood.

"You're a very beautiful man," she murmured, and spread her arms and legs in invitation. "Come here, beautiful man, and make me feel good."

"This first." He rolled on a condom, then lay beside her and leaned on an elbow so he could see her face. "Why are you acting this way?"

"Who says I'm acting?"

"Andrea, I'm not stupid. I tell you I love you, and your response is to entice me into your bed?" He stuck a finger into a curl near her ear and wound it around and around. "Don't you love me?" he whispered, afraid of the answer he might get.

She slid her hands up his chest and clasped them together behind his head. "Kiss first, talk later."

He kissed her as though trying to install the love he felt from his system to hers. She kissed him back in the same impassioned way. Their tongues met, and the kiss became hungry and needful.

She writhed beneath the caresses of his hands. It was still a contest of sorts, but they both knew they would each come out a winner. In this, in bed and making love, they were perfect together.

"I love you," Shep whispered raggedly against her lips.

"Now I believe you," she whispered back.

"Are you saying you didn't believe me before?"

"Shep, I think the word *love* means different things to us. You love me when I'm in your arms. Everywhere else, you don't trust me. You think I'm odd."

He couldn't hold back a small chuckle. "You are odd, sweetheart, but that doesn't stop me from loving you."

"I am *not* odd! Which you would know by now if you had let me explain about my notebook."

"I don't care about that damned notebook. I care about you."

To hell with it, she thought. She may as well find out how sincere he was, once and for all. "Do you want to marry me?" she asked.

"Uh . . . marry?"

"Got you there, didn't I?" She attempted to slide out from under him with the intention of getting off the bed. He didn't love her the way she loved him; there was very little similarity in what they felt for each other, and it hurt, even though she herself had caused the truth to come out.

But he moved fast and held her down. "No way, baby," he told her. "I'm here strictly by invitation, and I fully intend to finish what you started."

"Even if I've changed my mind?" she said coldly.

"Oh? You've changed your mind? Let's find out if that's true." Dipping his head, he began licking her right nipple. It became rigid at once, and he teased the tender bud with his tongue until he heard a whimper in her throat. Then he did the same with her other breast.

"You... have to... stop... doing that," she stammered hoarsely, breathlessly.

His response to her demand was to lick his way down her tummy. And then his face was between her legs, and she would have shrieked long and loudly if he had tried stopping.

She twined her fingers into his hair, closed her eyes and moaned in supreme pleasure. When she couldn't lie still, Shep moved up her body, kissed her mouth and then looked into her eyes. "Still want me to stop?"

Her head moved back and forth on the pillow. "No."

"Then you won't mind my doing this." Gently he slid his manhood inside of her and began moving it in and out, all the time watching her face. "Tell me you don't love me," he whispered thickly.

"I... can't."

"Then tell me you *do* love me."

"I love you."

"I knew it all the time," he muttered, burying his face in the pillow next to her head and forgetting everything but the intense pleasure of making love to her.

As had happened with them each time they'd made love before, they climaxed at almost the same moment. Weak and sated, they lay without moving for a long time.

Shep spoke first. "Guess I will marry you."

"*What?*"

He raised his head and grinned at her. "I said—"

"I heard what you said, but why did you say it? Do you think I would marry a man *I* had to propose to?"

Shep's grin disappeared. "You're kidding, right?"

"Are you or are you not disenchanted with the mere idea of marriage? Tell me the truth."

"You want the truth? Fine, let's talk." Shep rolled to the bed. "You will excuse me for a minute, won't you?" Getting off the bed, he left the room.

Andrea sighed, but then she hugged herself. What a day this had been. Oh, she had so much to tell Shep. If he ever let her do it, that is, she amended wryly.

But apparently he intended to talk about himself, and she wanted to hear what he had to say as badly as she wanted to open up with him.

Sitting up, she fluffed her hair with her fingers, then straightened the blankets. She was lying down again when Shep returned.

"Is it all right if I join you?" he asked.

"Since when do you ask?" she retorted pertly.

He laughed and climbed in beside her, burrowing one arm beneath her head and wrapping the other around her waist. "Are you intimating that I've had my way with you—how many times?—and never asked?"

"Bingo."

"Do you want me to ask from now on?"

"Is there going to be a 'from now on' for us?"

"There is as far as I'm concerned. Andrea, when I left California I vowed I would never get married again. I felt that one fiasco per person was enough, but I was equally certain I would never fall in love again."

"You did love your wife, then?"

"I thought so, yes. Since I met you..." Shep took a breath. "I don't know now. What I believed was love before is nothing like what I feel for you." He cocked his head to look into her eyes. "It happened fast, didn't it?"

"It happened the second you walked into this house on Christmas Day," she said softly.

He fell silent and finally asked, "You fell in love with me that quickly?"

"At first sight. Shep, what went through your mind when you first saw me?"

He chuckled in a completely masculine fashion. "That I'd like to get into your panties."

"You dog!" She whacked him on the arm. "Was that really your first thought?"

"Sure was. And I kept thinking it all through dinner, and later, when I came back and we ate supper."

"So I was right. Love and sex are the same thing in your dirty mind," she fumed.

"With you they are. What can I say? Do you hate me for it?"

Sighing, she draped her arm around his neck and hugged him. "I couldn't hate you for any reason."

"Sweetheart, do you want to hear about my marriage and divorce?"

She marveled at her change of heart, because she'd been dying to hear the gory details and now she couldn't care less. He loved her, not his ex-wife, and that was all she needed to know. "Not now. Maybe someday."

They lay quietly for a while, then Andrea shifted her position to face him. "I'm going to tell you about my notebook now, and don't you dare say you won't listen."

"You don't have to do this, Andrea. As you said, everyone's entitled to privacy."

"Which I still believe, but that notebook is no longer a private matter. Shep..." She was all but bursting with joy, and it showed on her face.

"Honey, what is it?"

"Shep...Charlie Fanon is my father!"

Epilogue

It was decided that the family would congregate at Charlie's house four nights later. Charlie called Andrea and told her that everyone was very anxious to meet her.

"Dad, is it all right if I bring a friend?" Andrea asked. It was such a thrill to just say the word *Dad* that Andrea felt tears in her eyes.

"A friend, honey?"

"The man I'm going to marry, Dr. Shepler Wilde."

"Well, of course it's all right to bring your fiancé. 'Wilde' is his last name? Is he related to Lucas Wilde, by any chance?"

"He's Lucas's son."

"I'll be danged, a hometown boy. And he's a doctor. Seems like I recall someone mentioning that a while back. The girls are putting together a buffet supper, so come around six. Oh, is six all right? I mean, with your working hours?"

"Six is fine. Shep and I will be there. Dad...is...is Serena all right?"

"Serena's fine, honey. You'll see for yourself."

After goodbyes, Andrea put down the phone and looked at Shep. "I should have asked if you'd go with me before committing you to a family evening. I'm sorry."

"Don't be. I want to go with you." Shep reached across the table for her hand. They were partially dressed, just enough for decency's sake while they ate a quickly put together supper. After the shock of Andrea's announcement had sunk in, Shep had been eager to hear her story, and she'd been just as eager to relate it. Several hours later, they'd realized that they were both ravenously hungry. Hopping out of bed, they had thrown on a few clothes and gone to the kitchen to scare up what they could from Andrea's diminished food supply.

It hadn't mattered what was on the table, however. There was so much excitement and happiness in that little kitchen, a simple supper certainly couldn't mar it. Shep had called Lucas only minutes before Charlie's call, and Lucas had been beside himself over the news of their engagement.

"You do realize something, don't you?" Shep asked his beloved while squeezing her hand.

"What's that?"

"Once we're married, you're going to have two fathers."

"Oh, Shep, you're right!" Tears sprang to her eyes. "Lucas and Charlie. I'm the luckiest woman alive."

But she hadn't always been so fortunate, and Andrea remembered the past and worried about the family evening every day at work. Juggling that concern while trying to concentrate on the newspaper—very exciting, incidentally—kept her mind so occupied that the days flew by.

Her worry intensified during the drive home to pick up Shep on the appointed evening for the Fanon family gathering. It was only natural for Charlie's family to want to meet her right away, but there were no guarantees that they weren't pulling the wool over Charlie's eyes just a little by pretending they were as thrilled with her intrusion into the inner circle as he was.

The truth was that she was a bundle of nerves over meeting everyone, especially Serena. Poor Charlie had had to tell his daughter that he'd lied about her mother, and it would take a very broad-minded woman indeed to instantly forgive and forget. Andrea knew she was going to be a reminder of Charlie's far-reaching lie, and not only that, Andrea had grown up with Sandra and Serena had not. It wouldn't be abnormal for Serena to harbor some resentment toward Andrea over that.

Shep was a dear during the drive to Charlie's home, trying to ease her distress with jokes and hospital anecdotes. They were almost there when Shep became serious.

"Andrea, I've been thinking about something all day."

"So have I, believe me."

"This is about me. Rather, it's about us. I'd like to open my own practice, but to do so I would have to go into debt. I wouldn't specialize. That is to say, I would practice as a G.P. with a surgical specialty. Not cosmetic reconstruction, honey, as I've always wanted to concentrate on accident victims and those unfortunate people with congenital defects. There would be a lot of equipment to buy, and while I have A1 credit, I don't have much cash. Starting our marriage with a huge debt load could be tough, so if you have any objections..."

Andrea turned in the seat to peer at him in the lights of the dash. "I am so proud of you I could cry. By all means, open your own practice." She was about to offer him every penny of her inheritance to get started when a brand-new thought knocked her for a loop. "Shep, stop the car."

"What?"

"Please pull over. I have to talk to you about something, and we're almost there."

"Well, sure, honey." With a worried glance at Andrea, he pulled into the plowed parking area of a roadside restaurant. Putting the shifting gear in Park, he turned to face her. "Now, tell me what's wrong?"

"It's my inheritance."

"I didn't know you had one. What about it?"

"It's not all mine! Don't you see? Mother had two other children. Her estate should have been split three ways."

Shep nodded. "You're right."

Andrea bit her lip. "How could she have put Serena and Ron so completely out of her life? Shep, I've tried very hard not to think of Mother as selfish, but how can I help it? She left two small children and apparently never gave them another thought. I . . . I just can't comprehend it."

"Of course you can't. But that's because you have more of Charlie's traits than hers."

Andrea's eyes misted. "Oh, I hope that's true. I've been thinking that Serena might resent me for having grown up with Mother, but she was the lucky one, Shep, not me."

"Yes," he said. "She was. Now, stop fretting about it. You can see a lawyer and have the estate divided."

Andrea smiled, albeit wanly. "Serena's a lawyer. I'm sure she can handle the details."

"I'm sure she can." Shep leaned across the seat and kissed her. "Shall we go and meet your family now?"

Andrea nodded, and Shep got underway again. "One thing more, darling. While my inheritance will be greatly diminished by a three-way split, I want you to use my third to start your practice."

"No, Andrea. I'd much rather borrow the money from the bank."

"But that doesn't make sense. We wouldn't have to start our marriage in debt."

"That's true, but I would always feel financially indebted to you. Honey, let me do this on my own, and don't let your feelings get hurt by it, either." He was silent a moment, then continued in a quieter tone. "I let Natalie's father finance my practice in L.A., Andrea. It was an enormous mistake."

"But I'm not Natalie, Shep," she said softly.

He took his eyes off the road to send her a loving glance. "You sure aren't, thank God."

"You must let me help you, Shep, you just have to. Oh, there's Charlie's house." Her stomach was suddenly in a knot. There were three strange vehicles parked in Charlie's driveway, but they were crammed in so that there was room for one more. Shep pulled into the space and turned off the ignition.

The last thing Andrea did before they got out was to clutch Shep's hand and whisper, "I'm terrified, Shep."

Since Shep had to be at work at eleven, they left Charlie's home at ten. Andrea had stars in her eyes. "They're wonderful, every one of them. Oh, Shep, they were all so kind to me."

"As they should be."

"Serena and I are going to meet for lunch tomorrow. She said she wants to know me better."

Shep already knew that, but he smiled and nodded. "She's a nice woman."

"And so are Lola and Candace. And their husbands. Did you like their husbands?"

"I remember Duke from years ago, honey. Liked him then and still do. Burke and Trav are great guys. Yes, I like all the husbands."

"And did you ever see a sweeter child than Ronnie?"

"Never, honey, never."

Andrea sighed happily. After a few moments, she spoke again. "I still can't believe they refused any part of Mother's estate." She frowned. "That's not true. If I were them, I wouldn't take it, either."

"Neither would I," Shep agreed. "Sandra wanted no part of them, and now they want no part of her. Don't blame them a bit. In fact, I like and admire their pride."

Andrea sent him a look. "Let's talk about *your* pride."

"Andrea, I'm not using any of your money. It would cause trouble between us, I guarantee it. Maybe not next week or even a year from now. But someday you would resent my spending your money."

"Okay, then how about a loan?"

"A loan?"

"Borrow from me instead of the bank. We're intelligent enough to work out reasonable terms, Shep. And you wouldn't feel indebted to me, and I would never have reason for resentment."

He cast her a glance. "You're a pretty smart cookie, do you know that?"

"Then you'll do it?"

"I'll think about it."

Andrea unhooked her seat belt and slid across the seat to snuggle against him. "Latch the center one," Shep told her. "The roads are slick, and I don't want you in the emergency room tonight."

Obediently she hooked the lap belt around her, then snuggled against his shoulder again. "I can't believe everything turned out so well," she said with a long sigh of total contentment. "I have only one regret, that I didn't drive directly to Dad's house when I got to Rocky Ford last spring."

"Well, we all do what we have to, honey. Apparently, the time wasn't right then."

"I suppose not."

"Hey, sweet thing, how come some guy in California didn't nab you?"

Andrea shrugged her free shoulder. "Just didn't happen."

"Are you telling me you've never been in love before?"

She smiled teasingly. "By any chance, are you trying to worm the facts of my love life out of me?"

"Could be," Shep said with a small chuckle. "Seriously, it's darned hard to believe a woman like you didn't have droves of men after her."

"No droves," Andrea quipped. After a moment, she said, "There were a few men who were important for a while, but I never really fell in love and it never lasted."

"But you dated."

"Oh, sure. I was dating an actor when I left California."

"You're kidding. An actor?"

"Actually, he's a pretty nice guy. Once you get past his unbelievable vanity, that is. Hale has a good sense of humor and was fun to go out with."

Hale? Shep frowned. Where had he heard that name before?

Then he remembered. "What is Hale's last name?" he asked casually.

"Jackson. He's been in a few movies, so maybe you've seen him." Andrea jumped a foot when Shep roared with laughter. "Did I say something funny?"

Shep couldn't stop laughing and he pulled over to the side of the road to wipe his eyes.

"Shep, what on earth is so hilarious?" Andrea asked.

He finally calmed down enough to answer. "My ex-wife is dating your ex-boyfriend."

Andrea stared. "You're kidding. How do you know?"

"I talked to a friend in L.A. not too long ago. He never was known for his tact, and he said that he'd run into Natalie at a party. Before I could tell him I wasn't interested in anything Natalie was doing, he rambled on with information I let go in one ear and out the other. But now I remember it. Andrea, she was with an actor named Hale Jackson, and he has a part in her father's latest film."

"Well, good for Hale," Andrea declared.

"You don't see the humor in that arrangement?" Shep asked.

"Not really. The old saying about it being a small world is true, Shep." She nestled closer. "Besides, I'd rather think about us." Lifting her chin, she looked up at him. "Incidentally, in case you're wondering, I never slept with Hale."

Shep grinned. "I never would have asked, but thanks for the good news." He got his car moving again.

"Christmas lovers," Andrea murmured.

"Pardon? I didn't hear what you said."

"I said we were Christmas lovers. We met and fell in love on Christmas Day. That makes us Christmas lovers."

Shep nodded, then took his right hand off the steering wheel, put his arm around her and drew her even closer.

Tenderly his lips brushed her forehead. "I guess it does, sweetheart. I guess it does."

* * * * *

COMING NEXT MONTH

#1045 THE COFFEEPOT INN—Lass Small

January's *Man of the Month*, Bryan Willard, met the most alluring female he'd ever seen—who turned out to be his new boss. He agreed to show inexperienced Lily Trevor the ropes...but he hadn't planned on teaching her about love!

#1046 BACHELOR MOM—Jennifer Greene

The Stanford Sisters

Single mother Gwen Stanford's secret birthday wish was to have a wild romance. But when her handsome neighbor Spense McKenna offered to give her just that, was Gwen *truly* ready to throw caution to the wind and succumb to Spense's seductive charms?

#1047 THE TENDER TRAP—Beverly Barton

One night of uncontrollable passion between old-fashioned Adam Wyatt and independent Blythe Elliott produced a surprise bundle of joy. They married for the sake of the baby, but would these expectant parents find true love?

#1048 THE LONELIEST COWBOY—Pamela Macaluso

Rancher Clint Slade's immediate attraction to devoted single mother Skye Williamson had him thinking that she might be the woman to ease his lonely heart. But would Skye's six-year-old secret destroy their future happiness?

#1049 RESOLVED TO (RE) MARRY—Carole Buck

Holiday Honeymoons

After eleven years, ex-spouses Lucy Falco and Christopher Banks were thrown together by chance on New Year's Eve. It didn't take long before they discovered how steamy their passion still was....

#1050 ON WINGS OF LOVE—Ashley Summers

Katy Lawrence liked to play it safe, while pilot Thomas Logan preferred to take risks. Could Thomas help Katy conquer her fears and persuade her to gamble on love?

FAST CASH 4031 DRAW RULES
NO PURCHASE OR OBLIGATION NECESSARY

Fifty prizes of $50 each will be awarded in random drawings to be conducted no later than 3/28/97 from amongst all eligible responses to this prize offer received as of 2/14/97. To enter, follow directions, affix 1st-class postage and mail OR write Fast Cash 4031 on a 3" x 5" card along with your name and address and mail that card to: Harlequin's Fast Cash 4031 Draw, P.O. Box 1395, Buffalo, NY 14240-1395 OR P.O. Box 618, Fort Erie, Ontario L2A 5X3. (Limit: one entry per outer envelope; all entries must be sent via 1st-class mail.) Limit: one prize per household. Odds of winning are determined by the number of eligible responses received. Offer is open only to residents of the U.S. (except Puerto Rico) and Canada and is void wherever prohibited by law. All applicable laws and regulations apply. Any litigation within the province of Quebec respecting the conduct and awarding of a prize in this sweepstakes maybe submitted to the Régie des alcools, des courses et des jeux. In order for a Canadian resident to win a prize, that person will be required to correctly answer a time-limited arithmetical skill-testing question to be administered by mail. Names of winners available after 4/28/97 by sending a self-addressed, stamped envelope to: Fast Cash 4031 Draw Winners, P.O. Box 4200, Blair, NE 68009-4200.

OFFICIAL RULES
MILLION DOLLAR SWEEPSTAKES
NO PURCHASE NECESSARY TO ENTER

1. To enter, follow the directions published. Method of entry may vary. For eligibility, entries must be received no later than March 31, 1998. No liability is assumed for printing errors, lost, late, non-delivered or misdirected entries.
   To determine winners, the sweepstakes numbers assigned to submitted entries will be compared against a list of randomly pre-selected prize winning numbers. In the event all prizes are not claimed via the return of prize winning numbers, random drawings will be held from among all other entries received to award unclaimed prizes.

2. Prize winners will be determined no later than June 30, 1998. Selection of winning numbers and random drawings are under the supervision of D. L. Blair, Inc., an independent judging organization whose decisions are final. Limit: one prize to a family or organization. No substitution will be made for any prize, except as offered. Taxes and duties on all prizes are the sole responsibility of winners. Winners will be notified by mail. Odds of winning are determined by the number of eligible entries distributed and received.

3. Sweepstakes open to residents of the U.S. (except Puerto Rico), Canada and Europe who are 18 years of age or older, except employees and immediate family members of Torstar Corp., D. L. Blair, Inc., their affiliates, subsidiaries, and all other agencies, entities, and persons connected with the use, marketing or conduct of this sweepstakes. All applicable laws and regulations apply. Sweepstakes offer void wherever prohibited by law. Any litigation within the province of Quebec respecting the conduct and awarding of a prize in this sweepstakes must be submitted to the Régie des alcools, des courses et des jeux. In order to win a prize, residents of Canada will be required to correctly answer a time-limited arithmetical skill-testing question to be administered by mail.

4. Winners of major prizes (Grand through Fourth) will be obligated to sign and return an Affidavit of Eligibility and Release of Liability within 30 days of notification. In the event of non-compliance within this time period or if a prize is returned as undeliverable, D. L. Blair, Inc. may at its sole discretion award that prize to an alternate winner. By acceptance of their prize, winners consent to use of their names, photographs or other likeness for purposes of advertising, trade and promotion on behalf of Torstar Corp., its affiliates and subsidiaries, without further compensation unless prohibited by law. Torstar Corp. and D. L. Blair, Inc., their affiliates and subsidiaries are not responsible for errors in printing of sweepstakes and prizewinning numbers. In the event a duplication of a prizewinning number occurs, a random drawing will be held from among all entries received with that prizewinning number to award that prize.

SWP-S12ZD1

5. This sweepstakes is presented by Torstar Corp., its subsidiaries and affiliates in conjunction with book, merchandise and/or prize offerings. The number of prizes to be awarded and their value are as follows: Grand Prize — $1,000,000 (payable at $33,333.33 a year for 30 years); First Prize — $50,000; Second Prize — $10,000; Third Prize — $5,000; 3 Fourth Prizes — $1,000 each; 10 Fifth Prizes — $250 each; 1,000 Sixth Prizes — $10 each. Values of all prizes are in U.S. currency. Prizes in each level will be presented in different creative executions, including various currencies, merchandise, vehicles, merchandise and travel. Any presentation of a prize level in a currency other than U.S. currency represents an approximate equivalent to the U.S. currency prize for that level, at that time. Prize winners will have the opportunity of selecting any prize offered for that level; however, the actual non U.S. currency equivalent prize, if offered and selected, shall be awarded at the exchange rate existing at 3:00 P.M. New York time on March 31, 1998. A travel prize option, if offered and selected by winner, must be completed within 12 months of selection and is subject to: traveling companion(s) completing and returning a Release of Liability prior to travel; and hotel and flight accommodations availability. For a current list of all prize options offered within prize levels, send a self-addressed, stamped envelope (WA residents need not affix postage) to: MILLION DOLLAR SWEEPSTAKES Prize Options, P.O. Box 4456, Blair, NE 68009-4456, USA.

6. For a list of prize winners (available after July 31, 1998) send a separate, stamped, self-addressed envelope to: MILLION DOLLAR SWEEPSTAKES Winners, P.O. Box 4459, Blair, NE 68009-4459, USA.

EXTRA BONUS PRIZE DRAWING
NO PURCHASE OR OBLIGATION NECESSARY TO ENTER

7. The Extra Bonus Prize will be awarded in a random drawing to be conducted no later than 5/30/98 from among all entries received. To qualify, entries must be received by 3/31/98 and comply with published directions. Prize ($50,000) is valued in U.S. currency. Prize will be presented in different creative expressions, including various currencies, vehicles, merchandise and travel. Any presentation in a currency other than U.S. currency represents an approximate equivalent to the U.S. currency value at that time. Prize winner will have the opportunity of selecting any prize offered in any presentation of the Extra Bonus Prize Drawing; however, the actual non U.S. currency equivalent prize, if offered and selected by winner, shall be awarded at the exchange rate existing at 3:00 P.M. New York time on March 31, 1998. For a current list of prize options offered, send a self-addressed, stamped envelope (WA residents need not affix postage) to: Extra Bonus Prize Options, P.O. Box 4462, Blair, NE 68009-4462, USA. All eligibility requirements and restrictions of the MILLION DOLLAR SWEEPSTAKES apply. Odds of winning are dependent upon number of eligible entries received. No substitution for prize except as offered. For the name of winner (available after 7/31/98), send a self-addressed, stamped envelope to: Extra Bonus Prize Winner, P.O. Box 4463, Blair, NE 68009-4463, USA.

As seen on TV!
Free Gift Offer

With a Free Gift proof-of-purchase from any Silhouette® book,
you can receive a beautiful cubic zirconia pendant.

This gorgeous marquise-shaped stone is a genuine cubic
zirconia—accented by an 18" gold tone necklace.

(Approximate retail value $19.95)

Send for yours today...
compliments of ▼ *Silhouette*®
™

To receive your free gift, a cubic zirconia pendant, send us one original proof-of-
purchase, photocopies not accepted, from the back of any Silhouette Romance™,
Silhouette Desire®, Silhouette Special Edition®, Silhouette Intimate Moments®
or Silhouette Yours Truly™ title available in August, September, October, November and
December at your favorite retail outlet, together with the Free Gift Certificate, plus a
check or money order for $1.65 U.S./$2.15 CAN. (do not send cash) to cover postage and
handling, payable to Silhouette Free Gift Offer. We will send you the specified gift. Allow
6 to 8 weeks for delivery. Offer good until December 31, 1996 or while quantities last.
Offer valid in the U.S. and Canada only.

Free Gift Certificate

Name: _____

Address: _____

City: _____ State/Province: _____ Zip/Postal Code: _____

Mail this certificate, one proof-of-purchase and a check or money order for postage
and handling to: SILHOUETTE FREE GIFT OFFER 1996. In the U.S.: 3010 Walden
Avenue, P.O. Box 9077, Buffalo NY 14269-9077. In Canada: P.O. Box 613, Fort Erie,
Ontario L2Z 5X3.

FREE GIFT OFFER   084-KMD
ONE PROOF-OF-PURCHASE
To collect your fabulous FREE GIFT, a cubic zirconia pendant, you must include this
original proof-of-purchase for each gift with the properly completed Free Gift Certificate.

084-KMD-R

You're About to Become a

Privileged Woman

Reap the rewards of fabulous free gifts and benefits with proofs-of-purchase from Silhouette and Harlequin books

Pages & Privileges™

It's our way of thanking you for buying our books at your favorite retail stores.

✂

PROOF OF PURCHASE

SD-PP20

Offer expires March 31, 1997

Pages & Privileges ™

Harlequin and Silhouette— the most privileged readers in the world!

For more information about Harlequin and Silhouette's **PAGES & PRIVILEGES** program call the Pages & Privileges Benefits Desk: 1-503-794-2499

Silhouette®

™

SD-PP20